DEBRA WEBB

Man of Her Dreams

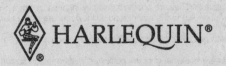

HARLEQUIN®

TORONTO • NEW YORK • LONDON
AMSTERDAM • PARIS • SYDNEY • HAMBURG
STOCKHOLM • ATHENS • TOKYO • MILAN • MADRID
PRAGUE • WARSAW • BUDAPEST • AUCKLAND

ISBN 0-373-88623-3

MAN OF HER DREAMS

www.eHarlequin.com

Printed in U.S.A.

ABOUT THE AUTHOR

Debra Webb was born in Scottsboro, Alabama, to parents who taught her that anything is possible if you want it badly enough. When her husband joined the military, they moved to Berlin, Germany, and Debra became a secretary in the commanding general's office. By 1985 they were back in the States, and with the support of her husband and two beautiful daughters, Debra took up writing full-time and in 1998 her dream of writing for Harlequin came true. You can write to Debra with your comments at P.O. Box 64, Huntland, Tennessee 37345 or visit her Web site at www.debrawebb.com to find out exciting news about her next book.

CAST OF CHARACTERS

Aidan—An Enforcer, a genetically engineered seer assigned to complete the Prophecy Mission.

Darby Shepard—A simple schoolteacher who has unexplainable dreams. But if she's so simple, why is her life in danger?

Madam Talia—A local New Orleans psychic. Can she help Darby discover the truth before it's too late?

Detective Lance Willis—He has to nail the serial killer who has been preying on children. Can Darby help him bring the man to justice?

Jerry Lester—A twisted murderer who is obsessed with children.

Howard Thomas—The Shepard family attorney. Does he know more about Darby's adoption than he's telling?

Director Richard O'Riley—Center Director. He has the power to order Darby's elimination. Will his conscience let him do what's best for Center?

Governor Kyle Remington—The new head of the Collective. The man in charge of the Collective has traditionally left the day-to-day operations to O'Riley. Will Remington prove a more forceful leader than his predecessor?

Dr. Waylon Galen—The creative mind behind the Enforcers. Will he win this time?

Wizard—Darby's cat.

Prologue

Ring a-round the roses,
Pocketful of posies

Her mother watched from the kitchen window as six-year-old Christina Fairgate frolicked in the backyard. She clutched her favorite doll under one arm and skipped around the circle she had made in the grass with the other dolls and stuffed animals from her room. She sang the nursery rhyme over and over, as if she expected her audience to join her.

The autumn Louisiana sun hovered like a glimmering orange in the western sky. Its golden rays were still powerful enough to force a sweat even as it slipped downward in surrender to the coming dusk.

Christina's mother smiled at the pleasant scene, then turned back to the oven to check on the special treat she had prepared for her daughter. One hand gloved with a thick mitt, she opened the oven door and removed the baking pan, allowing the delicious smell of homemade chocolate chip cookies to fill the air.

A sound of approval on her lips, she set the pan aside so the cookies would cool. After turning off the oven she poured her daughter, as well as herself, a cool glass of milk. A little snack this close to dinner wouldn't hurt. Handling the still warm dessert gingerly, she loaded a small plate with cookies and placed it on a tray, along with the two glasses of milk. No need for napkins. Licking gooey chocolate from fingers was part of the fun of homemade cookies.

But neither of them would ever taste those lovingly prepared cookies for when she made her way to the backyard with the laden tray, her little girl was gone.

Days would turn into weeks and weeks to a month before the body would be found.

Ashes, ashes,
We all fall down.

Chapter One

New Orleans
Two months later

They were coming for her.

Another test, more poking and prodding.

She couldn't let them know. If they ever found out what she could do…

Block the dreams. Don't look. Don't see.

They could never know the truth.

The man in the white lab coat smiled down at her. He spoke of his own daughter. He seemed kind. Much kinder than the other one. But she knew better than to trust even him. He wanted to know the truth so he could tell the others. And she would never be safe, never be free if they knew the truth.

It didn't matter that they'd held her prisoner her whole life, even before she was born. She could see beyond the walls, beyond the hiding place where they conducted their secret tests. She knew the truth.

But they could never know.

Never, never, never.

If they knew they would keep her forever.

Darby Shepard bolted upright in her bed. Her breath came in ragged gasps. She shoved her sweat-dampened hair from her eyes and forced her respiration to slow.

She was safe.

At home.

In her own bed.

No need to be afraid.

Long minutes passed before her racing heart calmed. She hated those dreams. Shivering with the receding adrenaline, she cursed herself as she stumbled out of bed. 7:00 a.m. already. She had to hurry or she'd be late for school.

As she quickly showered and then dressed, she tried repeatedly to put the dream out of her thoughts but she couldn't. It was always the same. The men in the white lab coats were coming for her. She had to keep her dreams a secret. Could tell no one. Couldn't tell them what she saw. She paused, her fingers stilling on the buttons of her dress. The part that got to her the most was the idea that the dream was a little too real.

She never told anyone what she saw in those nightmares. Never shared the dreams that came, unbidden, with another living soul for fear of…what? The men in the white coats? Maybe.

Darby quickly brushed her damp hair and twisted it into a braid. There was no time to dry the waist-length tresses or even to grab a bite of breakfast. She would be late for school. What kind of example would the teacher set if she showed up late for school?

Teacher. She did so love her work, loved the children.

The crisp October morning sent goose bumps across her skin as she pedaled her bike as fast as she could, quickly moving from Cohn to Broadway and then along Sycamore Street. Halloween was scarcely more than a week away. The ghosts and goblins would be out well before then. Like the North Pole was to Santa, New Orleans was the home to Halloween and all sorts of other wicked things.

She bore to the right on South Claiborne Avenue, then took a hard right onto Jefferson. She scarcely had time to notice the eighteenth-century cobblestoned streets she loved or the tourists and fortune-tellers alike who were already moving about this morning. Soon the streets would be filled with vendors and leftover partygoers from the night before.

Usually she took her time, absorbing the ambience, the history and architecture that still fascinated her after a lifetime of exploration. New Orleans was the kind of place that one never tired of admiring. There was always some new aspect that drew one in, whether it was the varied architecture along the lushly landscaped streets or the ancient foreboding of the numerous cities of the dead. Or even the crumbling lanes and alleys in the less savory parts of town.

Good and evil shared this domain; only time would tell which would prove victorious. Or perhaps it was the ever-shifting balance that captivated visitors to this historical city.

Children between the ages of five and nine scurried through the towering main entrance of the Iris Goodman School as Darby swung off her bike and chained it to the rack near the front of the post-Civil War building. The prestigious elementary school had served this uptown neighborhood for nearly a hundred years and Darby for four. A private facility, the classroom sizes were small and the academic offerings large.

Her satchel banged against her thigh as she took the steps two at a time. She paused at the door and drew in a deep breath before entering the school. She did so love her position as kindergarten teacher. However, adopting the proper comportment was essential.

Inside the chatter and clatter made her smile. The smell of old books and history bolstered her sense of belonging. This was what she'd been born to do. Teaching the children…protecting them.

Uneasiness slid through her at that last thought. She swallowed back the anxiety that attempted to climb into her throat and strode determinedly to her room. Three or four of her charges were already storing backpacks in their cubbies.

"Good morning, boys and girls," Darby offered as she settled her bag on her desk.

"Morning, Ms. Shepard," echoed from the rear of the room.

Happiness bloomed in Darby's chest as she watched more little ones filter into the room, leaving moms and dads waving from the door. She wiggled her fingers at the proud parents and wondered how it felt to have a child, to love and cherish it. It must be so hard to leave them at school, especially in the beginning.

She wondered then if she would ever know that feeling. Could she ever trust anyone enough to share herself that way? The hollow feeling she always experienced at the thought of family, past and future, often made her wonder if something else was missing in her life. She'd read somewhere that one in eight pregnancies started out as twins. According to the research, the surviving twin always felt as if something were missing in his life. Maybe that was her problem. She definitely felt an unexplainable emptiness.

Dismissing the extreme line of thinking, she focused her attention on taking out the papers she'd graded the night before and preparing for class to begin. And people thought the kids were the only ones who had homework.

In five minutes, the bell would ring and the school day would officially begin. Twelve sets of parents had entrusted her with not only the safety of their offspring, but also with the task of teaching the children everything they would need to know to begin their journey through the coming school years. Considering some of the headlines of late, that was saying something.

"Have you heard?"

Darby looked up to find Sandra Paige from the kindergarten classroom across the hall rushing toward her. Sandra had been the first person to make her feel welcome when she started here four years ago. They'd been good friends since.

"Heard what?" Every instinct warned Darby that she did not want to hear whatever her friend and co-worker had to say but there was no way to avoid it. It was the bane of the white-collar world: gossip.

Her face pale and her eyes wide with worry, Sandra ushered Darby into the corner farthest from where her students still lollygagged around their storage cubbies.

"A third child has gone missing," Sandra whispered, her voice as frantic as the worry in her eyes.

A peculiar stillness fell over Darby. Images flashed through her mind but she blocked them, refused to look. "Who was she?"

"Allison Cook from over at Isidore Newman." Sandra frowned. "How did you know it was a girl?"

It had started with Christina Fairgate. In the three weeks since her body had been discovered, two more children had gone missing, one boy and one girl. So far, the police were stumped as to finding a connection among the three. There were no matching details whatsoever. Two were from wealthy families, the other from a single mother living in the projects. One black, two whites. Approximate age was all the three had in common, discounting the events surrounding their disappearances, of course. In each case, the child had been at home playing in his or her own backyard with one parent or both inside the house.

Darby swallowed hard, then shrugged stiffly. "Just a guess." To stall her friend's inquisition, she quickly asked, "They still don't have any leads? No witnesses? Nothing?"

Sandra shook her head in weary resignation. "According to her mother, one minute she was there, the next she was gone. In broad daylight, just like the others."

The scent of home-baked chocolate chip cookies abruptly filled Darby's nostrils. The image of a little blond-haired girl skipping around in circles flashed before her eyes. *Ring a-round the roses. Pocketful of posies.*

Darby slammed the door on the other images and sounds that tried to intrude. She would not look, refused to see. From the moment Christina Fairgate's body had been found, she'd experienced those images...the smells. She didn't want to see. God, she didn't want to know.

"Are you all right?"

The sound of her friend's voice jerked her back to the here and now.

"Fine." She blinked. "I'm fine."

Sandra nodded, her expression thoroughly unconvinced. "Ooookay," she said, dragging out the syllable. "I have to get back to my classroom. I'll talk to you later."

Darby managed a nod. More like a twitch.

Another child had gone missing.

Two in the space of as many weeks.

Where are the others?

The question slammed into her brain, sent a wave of adrenaline surging through her veins.

There were others. The police just didn't know yet. Five or six, more maybe. She'd sensed it from the beginning. Why were the sensations coming now? Why couldn't she make it stop? Or learn something useful from it?

The bell rang, jerking her from the troubling thoughts and sending students scurrying for their seats. Darby moistened her lips and manufactured a smile. Using every ounce of strength she possessed, she directed her attention to her class. "Let's get settled, girls and boys." She paused long enough for two stragglers to make their way to their seats. "Today is Monday," she continued when all eyes were focused on her. "Let's talk about what makes Mondays special."

Even at five, the children knew there was absolutely nothing special about Mondays.

AT 4:30 P.M., Darby slowed the momentum of her bike in front of an antebellum home in the Lower Garden District. She stopped on the side of the street, propping her weight against the curb with her right foot, keeping her left on the pedal to facilitate a hasty departure.

Corinthian fluted columns supported the home's double gallery. Floor-to-ceiling windows allowed the last of the sun's warming rays to tumble across its floors. She didn't have to get off her bike and walk to the rear of the property to know that lovely gardens, bordered by brick walks with a bubbling fountain in the center, graced the backyard. Though sorely out of place in its nineteenth-century setting, a colorful metal swing set— red, yellow and blue—stood proudly in the middle of it all.

Yellow crime scene tape sprawled across the front of the property, flapping in the wind, its middle sagging and giving the appearance of a sinister smile.

This was the home where Allison Cook lived…the yard where she'd been playing when she disappeared.

A shadow moved through the lush shrubbery. Male, she knew, but she couldn't see his face. Yet his voice was familiar. She heard that raspy, evil voice in her dreams. *No one can save the children. They belong to me. One, two, I'm coming for you. Three, four, better lock your door.*

Darby shuddered, pushed the voice away. She stared at the bushes where her mind had conjured the image of the shadow. Did the police know that he'd been hiding there? He'd watched until it was safe to grab the little girl. She concentrated hard, tried to see how he'd hushed the child. An inhalant. Quick, painless. The child would slump helplessly in his arms.

Her fingers tightened on the handlebars. How long did he watch the children before he made a move? Where did he take them afterwards? If she could see, if she dared to really look, maybe she could save the ones who weren't dead…yet.

The latest victim was still alive, but she couldn't sense anything definite about the others.

"Move along, ma'am."

Darby jumped at the sound of the harshly barked order. Uniformed policeman. NOPD.

"This isn't a sideshow," he snapped impatiently. "Have some respect for the family. Now move along!"

Darby blinked, dragged her sluggish mind from the trance she'd slipped into. She had to go. The realization that a cop was speaking to her, the visual implications of his uniform and the cruiser parked a few feet away, suddenly cracked through the haze.

"I'm sorry…I…" She looked back at the house one last time. The sound of weeping, the weight of overwhelming anguish, abruptly echoed through her soul.

"Let's see some ID."

Another voice.

Male.

Darby's gaze collided with dark brown eyes that were methodically sizing her up. The eyes belonged to a man dressed in a suit. A cop, too, she realized when he flashed his badge.

"I'm Detective Willis. Let's see some identification, ma'am."

Still feeling dazed, she fumbled in her satchel for her wallet. She showed him her driver's license and waited for him to ask the questions that would come next.

"Ms. Shepard, what brings you to this neighborhood?"

He wouldn't want to hear the truth. "I was on my way home." She mentally grappled for an excuse to be on this street. "I thought I'd stop by Sardi's Deli." She knew the place. It was only a few blocks away. Though there were delis close to home, he couldn't prove that she hadn't been headed to this particular one for one reason or another.

He studied her a moment longer as she put her wallet away. She could feel him assessing her, deciding if her excuse was legitimate or warranted further questioning.

Realization struck her then. They were desperate for a lead in this case. They were hoping the perpetrator would show up at the scene of the crime again. Perhaps to get a look at the grieving parents. He would so love that. *The children belonged to him now.*

Her senses went on alert as the detective reached into the interior pocket of his jacket. She held very still so as not to give away her edginess. When his hand came back into view, he held a small white business card.

"Why don't you call me if you think of anything from your observations that might assist us in this case." The statement was made grudgingly, but the look of desperation in his eyes didn't back up his indifferent tone.

Darby reached for the card, her fingers brushed his and in that one instant she felt his pain, his fear. Fear that he wouldn't be able to solve this mystery. Pain at having watched the autopsy of one dead child, fear that another might follow soon.

She nodded. "Sure," was all she could manage.

Pushing off with her left foot, she sped away from the Cook home and the lawmen stationed there. Four children…one found murdered. How many more would be sacrificed before they stopped this madman?

Trying hard to think of anything but those helpless children, Darby rushed home, pushing herself to the limit. By the time she reached Cohn Street, her legs ached, her lungs burned. She lugged her bike onto the porch that fronted the shotgun house she called home. The place had been divided into two apartments. Hers was the one-bedroom on the left side. Her neighbor, a stewardess who spent a lot of time away from home, occupied the two-bedroom on the right. The place had a small but nice yard that the landlord went to great lengths to keep looking sharp. He'd won the city's beautification award for rental property several years running. Inside, hardwood floors, ancient yet well-maintained fixtures and a gas fireplace provided the primary details Darby had been looking for when she found the place.

She unlocked the door and stepped inside the cool dark interior. Wizard, her tomcat, met her at the door. He yowled and wound himself around her legs, tail twitching. Darby tossed her satchel aside and ushered Wiz out the door. She'd had him neutered long ago so he wouldn't wander far.

Without bothering with lights, she went straight to her bedroom to change out of "teacher" wear. Jeans and T-shirts were her preferred attire.

I'm coming for you.

The words whispered through the darkness, sending fear snaking around her chest.

Darby closed her eyes and forced all thought of the missing children from her mind. This was why she never looked, never allowed herself to see. Once it got started, she couldn't stop it. She couldn't let the visions…the dreams…take control of her life. Not again. She'd allowed that to happen once. Thank God she'd still been at home with her parents then. They'd protected her. But there was no one to protect her now.

Better lock your door.

Darby turned on the shower, stripped off her clothes and stepped beneath the spray of water. She focused on the feel of the hot water pelting her skin. She blocked all other sensory perception. She would not see, would not hear. There was nothing she could do to help those children. The dreams were never complete. Just enough information came to torture her with sounds and sensations. Never enough to help. It had always been that way.

And even if she could see, how would she ever convince the police to believe her?

She had to let it go. There wasn't enough information to make a difference. She sensed snippets, voices, images, but there were never sufficient pieces of the puzzle to put it together. Back in junior high school, when her parents had spent the weekend coddling her after a fierce "dream" episode, she had promised herself she would never let the dreams take control again. The record of her "episode" was no doubt included in her school transcript. *Crazy. Out of control. Talking nonsense.*

The episodes had always been there, even before her real life had begun. Darby braced her hands against the slick tile walls and thought back to her early childhood. That place. The white lab coats and the constant poking and prodding. The only thing she could figure out from that time was that she'd been a part of some sort of experiment. She'd lived at this place hidden away in the mountains. A hospital or clinic. They'd called it *Center.* She remembered the word, the place, but not in detail.

Her gut told her she'd been born there and would never have escaped if she hadn't played the game she'd devised. Fear knotted inside her at even the thought of being back there again. She had known somehow, had sensed, that her future depended upon her *not* being able to perform as they required. All she'd had to do was pretend she didn't see, that she didn't understand.

When all means to prompt what the men in the white lab coats had obviously thought to be her hidden talent failed, they had sent her away.

At first, she hadn't been able to remember Center or the men in the white coats. She'd been adopted by a nice family in New Orleans, the Shepards, and for a while she'd drifted in a sea of nothingness. It was as if she'd been born the day they brought her to their home. Only instead of being an infant, she'd been ten years old. Gradually, a few meager memories of her time before had come to her in dreams and visions, the very ones she struggled not to see to this day.

As a result of the intense episode in her junior high days, her adopted parents had insisted that she be evaluated. The evaluation had shaken loose even more of her hidden past, but she'd never told anyone. The psychologist had considered her "episode" a traumatic event brought on by puberty and had prescribed medication. Darby had carried those tranquilizers with her since. Whenever she felt control slipping, she took them faithfully for a few nights. The nagging dreams would stop. Her refusal to look, enabled by the medication, kept her sane most of the time.

Now and again, the struggle to focus on the here and now rather than on some stranger's immediate past was nearly more than she could bear. The fight to keep the portal closed was a constant battle.

Darby twisted the knobs to the Off position and reached for her towel. Now, she decided, was a perfect time for that extra help. She'd been extremely lucky for several years now. She'd been able to control those heightened senses without the medication. But her usual means weren't working. The voices and images kept coming, tearing her apart and at the same time telling her nothing.

She couldn't risk another psychotic break like the one she'd experienced all those years ago. The adoptive parents who'd loved and cared for her were gone now, leaving her on her own. Alone with no protection, no support system.

She had to be strong, had to protect herself.

Wrapping the towel around her, she headed to the kitchen in search of the pills that would make the voices and images go away.

She filled a glass with water and unscrewed the childproof lid on the bottle. As much as she hated running from anything, she understood the necessity in this case. She couldn't lose control under any circumstances. There was no one to protect her from the voices and the images. No one to protect her from the men in the white lab coats.

If they learned where she was and that she had fooled them all those years ago, they would come for her. She knew things, though she didn't understand what any of it meant, that she shouldn't. With every fiber of her being, she felt certain that if they ever found out she had the dreams, they would come.

Better lock your door.

Chapter Two

Darby stared at the front page of the *Times-Picayune*.

Third Child Missing—Police Have No Leads.

She took another long drink of water in an attempt to dampen her dry mouth. The pills left her with cottonmouth as well as a heck of a hangover. But they worked. She hadn't dreamed at all last night. Even now, staring at the headline, she felt nothing. Numb maybe, but that didn't count.

Tossing the newspaper aside, she pushed to her feet and gathered her satchel. She hated the medication, hated this feeling of nothingness. But it was better than the alternative, wasn't it?

She dragged her fingers through her hair and sighed. Was it really? If she tried—really tried—could she see the man's face? Could she help those children, assuming either of the last two taken was still alive? She just didn't know. And, God, if she could help... she didn't even want to think that way. The little Fairgate girl was dead. No one could help her now.

Work. She needed work to distract her. Having managed to wake up on time this morning, she was actually a little ahead of schedule. She'd take the scenic route this morning. Get some fresh air and exercise. That would clear her head.

Feeling better already, Darby hung the long strap of her satchel over her head and onto the opposite shoulder so it wouldn't slip off and knock her off balance as she rode her bike. She said goodbye to Wiz and locked up her cozy apartment. After settling onto her bike, she took Broadway, then St. Charles over to Jefferson. The scenic route would be just the distraction she needed. She'd always loved the old homes and ancient live oaks that lined that street. There was just so much history there.

Darby wondered as she rode, the wind wafting her hair over her shoulders, if that's what made her feel so at home in New Orleans. The sense of history, of old souls hanging about. Some might find that odd, eerie even, but not Darby. She liked the feeling of being close to such a colorful and varied past.

There was no place in America like New Orleans.

When she'd been a teenager she'd sneaked into Lafayette Cemetery with some of her friends. The others had gotten spooked and ran for their lives, but she'd been enthralled with the City of the Dead. It had seemed mystical, healing. She hadn't felt the least bit frightened. Maybe because she understood the ambience there. She sensed the energy left behind by those who'd come before her. It wasn't good or evil spirits, as her friends had assumed. No ghosts. Just the essence left behind by all those souls who'd once walked this same earth. People had nothing to fear from the dead; it was the living who committed crimes.

Clairvoyance was vastly misunderstood, to Darby's way of thinking. Though she hadn't precisely studied it and definitely hadn't spoken to anyone about it, she understood her particular talent. Perhaps it was different for others. She possessed no ability to speak with the dead or even the living, other than by the usual means. She merely felt things on a much more heightened level than other humans. Sometimes she wondered if she actually was…human. The dreams she experienced at times reminded her of things that she'd seen in the movies. She wondered on those occasions just what they had done to her at that place…Center.

She shook off the silly notion. Yes, she was human. Her personal physician would vouch for that. Though she'd never been sick, she had had the required physicals throughout her life. When she thought about it, the idea that she'd never had the first virus or typical childhood illness could be seen as odd. Dr. Tygart simply chalked it up to good genes.

The memory of the one accident she'd had as a kid followed on the heels of that. She'd broken her arm falling from a tree. It had hurt for a day or two. Dr. Tygart had been amazed at how quickly she healed. Practically overnight. Again, he'd raved about how lucky she was to have inherited such excellent genetic traits.

She'd read about genetic manipulation, had heard about designer babies. Who hadn't? But she was twenty-six years old. Scientists hadn't had the technology to do such things that many years ago.

Frowning, Darby dismissed that line of thinking as well. Obsessing about her murky past was not the kind of distraction she'd had in mind this morning when she'd taken this longer route.

Directing her attention back to the lovely historic homes, she admired the craftsmanship and felt blessed that those with the money and wherewithal had chosen to maintain the beauty of the Old South. She'd even thought at one time of going into the antiques business with her mother. But after the accident, she just hadn't been able to bring herself to set foot back in that shop. Nor had she been able to sell it. So she leased the elegant Jackson Square shop and someone else made his living in antiques there. She'd closed up the big old house outside of town, promising herself she'd move there one day and have a large enough family to fill it. Every summer, she spent a couple of weeks in her parents' home, airing the place out and removing a year's worth of dust.

Even after five long years, she could still feel their presence there. Too strongly. Unlike the cemeteries, where the lingering essence of so many pressed in around her without disturbing her, this was different. It was deeply personal, more than she could bear. Maybe in time.

Darby stopped for a coffee and beignet. The powdered sugar melted in her mouth; the beignet tasted so good she had to lick her fingers. Feeling energized by the caffeine and sugar fix, she covered the rest of the journey in record time. The usual fortune-tellers, street charlatans and tourists had already gotten thick on the sidewalk.

She parked her bike and merged with a group of children to climb the massive stone steps to the school's front entrance. A smile moved across her face and she realized then and there that going back on the medication had been the right thing to do. She loved her work, loved her life; she didn't need the unnatural interference of the dreams. It would serve no purpose, since she had never once been able to harness the power she possessed and focus it precisely enough to make any sense of what she experienced.

Her so-called "gift" was useless.

Had she had any real talent, she might have prevented her parents from taking that weekend trip that took their lives. An unexpected college project was all that had prevented her from boarding that fishing boat with them.

What good was a gift if you couldn't help those you cared about?

The moment Darby entered the school's enormous main hall, a heavy weight settled upon her like a casket covered with shovelful after shovelful of graveyard dirt. Sadness. Desperation. Or a combination of the two. The halls and rooms were oddly quiet. Even the children seemed to rush to their rooms as if they'd felt the same dark weight as she.

Headmaster Theodore Yeager waited at her classroom door. Uneasiness crept up her spine, slowing her step as she neared him. Why would he be waiting at her door? Had a parent complained about her work? That didn't seem likely. She had a great relationship with all her parents. The children loved her. In the four years that she had worked here, she'd never had a single complaint.

"Good morning, Mr. Yeager. Is everything all right?" She studied his somber expression and even before he spoke, she knew the news was bad. Very bad.

"Ms. Shepard, let's step into your room."

She followed him inside, where he closed the door. Where were the children? Usually Anna or Tyler got to the room even before her. The sound of emptiness echoed around her, adding another layer of dread to her uneasiness.

"Your students are in Ms. Paige's room. I wanted to speak with you privately before class begins. I called you at home but you'd already left."

She had left a full thirty minutes early this morning. "What's wrong?" She couldn't bear not knowing any longer. A kind of mental darkness pressed against her mind…tried to show her something, but the medication was still working too well for it to get past.

"I'm so sorry to be the one to tell you this but little Anna Talbot went missing early this morning."

Denial broadsided Darby. "No." She shook her head. No. There had to be a mistake.

"I know how close you are to all your students, Ms. Shepard. They suspect the same person who has taken the other children. It's horrible…just horrible."

This couldn't be. She refused to believe. Her body started to shake. She couldn't control it. Tears flooded her eyes, making vision impossible. The next thing she knew, Mr. Yeager had guided her to the chair behind her desk.

"I'll have Ms. Paige keep your class until

you've composed yourself, Ms. Shepard. We don't want to frighten the children. This is so utterly horrible. I can hardly believe it myself. I—"

"How do they know it was him?"

Mr. Yeager frowned, stared at her as if from some far away place. "They…oh…they found the flowers…the…" He threw his hands up, flustered. "Whatever kind of flowers this monster leaves."

"Posies," she murmured. That's why at least one newspaper had dubbed him the Bouquet Killer. He always left a handful of crushed posies behind when he took the child. "They're sure it happened this morning?" she asked, suddenly remembering that the other three had gone missing just before sunset.

Headmaster Yeager nodded. "She went outside to get her lunchbox from the car. She'd forgotten to bring it inside last evening. Her mother said she'd only been gone a minute, maybe two, when she went to the door to see what was keeping her." He shook his head. "She just needed her lunchbox to prepare for school."

Darby stood. Her legs were still shaky but she had to pull herself back together. The other children needed her. She had to be strong for them. Poor Anna. A sob ripped at her chest. Poor…poor Anna.

The morning dragged into noon with no word from the Talbot family or the police. Darby had no appetite but she forced down a few bites during her lunch break to stave off the dizziness. The teachers speculated that all the Bouquet kidnappings would end in death. Darby scarcely kept her pitiful excuse for lunch down. Finally she excused herself and went back to her room early.

When the children were down for their afternoon nap, she propped her arms on her desk and laid her head there. God, she was so tired…and she couldn't get the image of sweet little Anna out of her mind. So smart. So pretty. Darby held back the tears, just barely. But a moment or two with her eyes closed would definitely be beneficial. Her eyes were red and tired from fighting tears all morning. She needed to rest them…just for a moment…

Ring a-round the roses.
Pocketful of posies.
Anna…Anna…I've got you, Anna.
He laughed long and loud, the sound pure

evil. His jaw was hard, scarred…a long, thin scar down his right cheek.

One, two, I'm coming for you. Three, four, better lock your door.

Darby tried to wake herself up, but she couldn't. She was trapped in the dream with…him. She could smell his sweat, could feel little Anna's fear. God, help her! She didn't want to see! No, please, she didn't want to see!

They belong to me now.

Darby jerked upright. Her breath whooshed out in a rush. She blinked twice and fought for her bearings.

Her classroom. She blinked again. The children were still sleeping.

She swiped at her wet cheeks. Anna. She closed her eyes and suppressed a sob. Dear, sweet little Anna.

Darby stilled. She'd heard his voice distinctly this time. Had even gotten a glimpse of his profile. A scar ran down the length of his cheek on the right side of his face. His nose was overlarge and his jaw flinty, hard.

For the first time in her life, she felt with a fair measure of certainty that this time she might see more. Her heart started to pound all over again. She surveyed the room. The few children whose parents hadn't picked them up after hearing the news slept soundly.

She could try. She dragged in a hollow breath. She had to try.

Darby closed her eyes and focused on the image of the man she'd seen in her dream. She prayed he was the one...the Bouquet Killer. If he was and she could see him more clearly, could make out details of where he was, then maybe she could help Anna and the others.

Please, God, she prayed, *let them still be alive.*

She had never tried to bring on a dream before, had never discussed the dreams at all with anyone—not even her parents after that one time. A part of her had been too afraid of the men in the white coats finding out. Some part of her had known with certainty that if they found out, they would come for her. So she kept her secret. But she had read about selfinduced hypnosis. So she started there.

Relaxing her muscles one by one, she lulled herself toward total relaxation. She pushed away all thought and opened her mind to the sensations around her. The smell of books and drying finger paint from the children's artwork. The soft snoring of one of the children. The hard feel of the wooden desk beneath her arms. The texture of her own skin where her cheek pressed against her forearm.

Light slashed through her brain, blinding in its intensity. Her respiration picked up, each breath harder than the last to draw into her lungs.

She could smell the water…the river. Rotting foliage. The grass was deep. No, not grass…weeds…underbrush. The woods. She was in the woods along the river. It was dark. She was alone. The ambient sounds of night echoed so loudly in her ears she wanted to scream, but she couldn't. If she screamed, he would know she was there.

A sound came from behind her. She stopped dead in her tracks. It came again. The brush of foliage against fabric. Someone was behind her…coming closer.

Darby turned around slowly, careful not to make a sound.

She sucked in a breath…sat straight up at her desk.

It was him.

She blinked.

Shook herself from the mist of sleep still clinging to her soul.

"Ms. Shepard!"

"Ms. Shepard, what's the matter?"

Darby blinked again and the children's faces came into focus. All six of those who remained in her class stood in front of her desk staring at her wide-eyed, fear dancing across their little faces.

"I'm fine," she said thickly. "Sorry. I'm fine."

Her fingers were clenched into fists. Her heart hammered in her chest.

"You kept jerking and wiggling," little Matt Caruthers told her. "My dog does that sometimes when he sleeps. Were you having a nightmare, Ms. Shepard?"

She nodded and forced her fingers to relax. "I guess so, Matt. I'm sorry. I didn't mean to frighten any of you."

Darby stood, smoothed her hands over her skirt and moved around her desk. "Let's read a story. Jenny, you choose this time."

For the rest of the afternoon Darby went through the motions. She read to the children and they talked about the different stories that each of them loved. But no matter how hard she tried, she couldn't keep those deep, dark woods out of her mind. She'd seen him there. Somewhere near the river. Of course, in New Orleans that could be a lot of places. But it was something.

For the first time in her life, she felt certain she could reach out and touch him...see what he saw. That's what she'd been doing in the dream. That's why he'd been behind her. She'd been seeing through his eyes part of the time.

But how much time did she have before he hurt one or all of the children? Could she spare the time it might take to focus her mind fully on his location?

Time was her enemy.

The children might not have time.

WHEN HER LAST STUDENT had gone, Darby rushed from the school without exchanging the usual pleasantries with her friends and co-workers. She had to hurry. She pedaled as fast as she dared in the afternoon traffic. She had made up her mind that she needed help for this. The kind of help only a selfprofessed psychic could give.

She'd heard the other teachers talk about Madam Talia. Some even admitted to having had their futures told by the woman. Madam

Talia had a reputation for being the best in New Orleans. One of those magazine talk shows had even done a special program on her. Darby wasn't exactly sure she believed in that sort of thing, but she didn't have anything to lose. If the woman knew anything at all about clairvoyance, she was way ahead of Darby. That was all that mattered at the moment.

Madam Talia's shop boasted a landmark location on the corner of Bourbon Street. Well, Darby deduced as she parked her bike on the sidewalk and locked it securely, at the very least the lady was making a living. She had to be doing something right. Surely Darby would sense if the woman was a fake.

There was only one way to find out.

An older woman dressed much like any typical receptionist met Darby in the small lobby. Surprisingly, the waiting room was decorated in an elegant and conservative manner. It was nothing like she'd expected.

"My name is Darby Shepard," she told the receptionist. "I'd like to see Madam Talia. It's very important."

The lady, who was dressed in just as quietly elegant a fashion as the office was decorated, smiled patiently. "I'm very sorry, Ms.

Shepard, but you'll need to make an appointment. Madam Talia is booked weeks in advance. She doesn't take walk-ins."

Darby's hopes fell. But she had to see her today. Desperation surged. "I'll only take a minute," she countered. "It's extremely important. I really need to see her today."

The woman looked sympathetic but said, "I sympathize with your urgency, but there's simply nothing I can do. Madam Talia is with a client as we speak and she expects her next appointment to arrive shortly."

Darby heaved a sigh. Oh well. The whole idea had been foolish anyway, she supposed. She'd just have to go home and see what she could do on her own.

"Thanks anyway," she offered, then turned to leave. Worry gnawed at her insides. She had to help those children. She should have tried before now, shouldn't have been such a coward. If something happened to them, it would be partly her fault for not trying to help sooner.

"Ms. Shepard."

Darby wheeled around at the sound of the new voice that called her name. Though she had never met Madam Talia, she knew instinctively that the refined lady who had addressed her was, indeed, the woman she wanted to see.

"Come this way, Ms. Shepard."

Unable to find her voice, Darby followed. The receptionist said nothing more as she resumed her seat behind her well-polished desk.

Madam Talia led Darby down a long narrow corridor and then into a small room that resembled the parlor in her mother's home. The upholstered furnishings were New Orleans red, the wood detailing a rich mahogany.

"Please make yourself comfortable," her hostess suggested with a wave of her arm.

Darby sat in one of the chairs flanking a small table. Madam Talia settled in the one adjacent to her.

"I've been wondering when I would meet you," she said to Darby.

Startled, Darby smiled. "I...I don't understand."

"I've always known you were here, Ms. Shepard," Madam Talia said. "I just didn't know why, but I think that's about to change."

Emotion surged into Darby's throat. She resisted the impulse to pinch herself to make sure she wasn't dreaming. "I need your help," she said tightly.

"You seek the children, do you not?"

Darby nodded. Tears stung her eyes. How could she know? She started to ask but changed her mind. It didn't matter. All that mattered was that she could help. Darby didn't have to wonder, she knew the answer, felt it to the very core of her being. This woman was the real thing.

"I've seen him," Darby whispered. "I just don't know how to focus. I don't know where he is." She shrugged. "The woods...water. I don't know."

"I've searched for him myself," Madam Talia admitted. "But he eludes me. But then you understand that, don't you?"

Darby shook her head. "I don't understand any of it."

The older woman took her hand. A rush of energy shot up to Darby's shoulder. She trembled at the intensity of it.

"We see what we're destined to see. At least most of us do. I'm not so sure about you. You've spent too much time block-ing...suppressing your gift. You may have a much larger gift than the rest of us."

Darby tried hard to restrain the shaking that

had started in her limbs, but she wasn't entirely successful. "I dream sometimes. See things that don't always make sense. That's all."

Madam Talia laughed softly. "You have no idea what you're capable of, my dear. You've come to me for guidance, for focus and yet you possess a gift far more powerful than my own." She reached for Darby's other hand. "Let us meditate a moment."

Madam Talia closed her eyes. Darby moistened her lips and tried to calm her racing heart, but that wasn't happening this side of the grave. Still uncertain of herself, she closed her eyes as well and tried to relax, tried to open her mind to the sensations she knew were out there…waiting.

Energy whirled around her…around them. She could feel its power; it was like standing too close to an electrical plant's substation and feeling the tiny hairs stand up on your skin.

The images came in clipped flashes, too fast to interpret. Fast and furious. Children, the woods, the water, the flowers growing in pots. Lots and lots of posies growing in pots on the porch of a dilapidated old shack. Near the water.

Her breath stalled in her lungs when she

looked directly into clear gray eyes. The scar stood out in stark relief on his cheek. The stubble of two days' beard growth darkened his jaw. He taunted the children, laughed at their cries.

Ring a-round the roses. Pocketful of posies.

Sensation after sensation slammed into Darby. She couldn't breathe, couldn't move, couldn't speak.

She was there.

The children.

Anna…the boy…and another girl.

But Darby had to hurry.

The hum of energy died as abruptly as it had started. Her eyes opened and Madam Talia stared directly at her.

"What did you see?" she asked, her voice weak, frail. She looked weary.

Had joining hands with Darby done that to her?

Suddenly the vision came back to her in one rapid whoosh. The cabin, the flower pots, the children.

"I know where they are."

The words were scarcely a whisper, a thought spoken.

Darby was on her feet before the command left her brain. She had to find them.

"No," Madam Talia said, her voice firm now, her expression hard. "You go to the police. Let them find the children. Do not go into the woods, Darby Shepard. Go home." Her eyes widened and she looked suddenly afraid. *"Better lock your door."*

FIFTEEN MINUTES LATER, Darby walked into the precinct office at Jackson Square. She remembered the detective who'd questioned her last evening. Still had his card.

Her movements awkward as if she no longer held dominion over her muscles, she walked up to the duty desk and said, "I need to see Detective Willis."

The uniformed sergeant didn't look up from the papers he was busily shuffling. "Detective Willis is a busy man. How can I help you?"

Darby moistened her lips and summoned her courage. The shaking wouldn't subside. She just couldn't stop it. "Please, sir, it's urgent that I speak with Detective Willis."

He looked up at her then. "Like I said, lady, it's me or nothing. Now, how can I help you?"

She took a breath, nodded stiffly. "All right…I… just…" Her gaze locked with his. "I think I know where the children are."

Chapter Three

Center
Ghost Mountain
Colorado

Governor Kyle Remington shook his head at the collection of newspapers on the conference table before him. Center and its advanced work were the most tightly kept secrets in the nation. How could this happen? "Tell us how this happened, Director O'Riley."

His gaze shifted from the dozen or so papers and settled solemnly onto Richard O'Riley. The other members of the Collective seated around the long conference table turned their attention in his direction as well. O'Riley was the man whose primary responsibility was to protect the nation's top scientific research facility.

"There is no easy explanation," O'Riley stalled. He had gotten the first ripples of intelligence on this matter at dawn this morning. Dupree, Center's senior intelligence analyst, had picked it up on the Net. Not the Net as in the Internet, but Center's Net, a specialized surveillance system that monitored all sources of mass communication— the World Wide Web, telephones, satellites and the like. Certain key words triggered the Net and the source of the key words was then recorded and analyzed for relevant data.

More than a dozen Louisiana newspapers had rushed to change copy at the crack of dawn to include a break in a big case involving missing children in New Orleans. By 7:00 a.m., every single one of those front pages had recounted a story right off the pages of a science fiction novel. Psychic Teacher Leads Police To Child Killer... Teacher Uses Special Gift To Find Missing Student...etcetera, etcetera.

Eve was all grown up.

For sixteen years, Center had assumed her case to be a failure. But now they knew differently.

The whole damned world knew differently.

"Darby Shepard, aka Eve, was deemed a failure sixteen years ago," O'Riley began. The impatient expressions pointed in his direction told him they wanted to hear something they didn't already know. "At age ten, after years of intensive training, she continued to show no progress. In fact, she became combative and uncooperative."

"Why was she not terminated?" a senior member wanted to know. "Isn't that the usual protocol for failures?"

O'Riley bit back the first response that raced to the tip of his tongue. "Yes. Termination is the standard protocol. However…" He wondered what he could possibly say that would make a difference. He looked from one face to the other. He had known the members of this elite committee for more than twenty years. They represented the most distinguished scholars, the most dedicated politicians, and still there were times when O'Riley wondered if it was enough. Was any mere human, or collective of the species, really qualified to make these kinds of ultimate decisions?

Maybe he was simply getting old and soft. Maybe he'd always secretly had a heart that wasn't completely made of stone. His ex-wife certainly wouldn't agree with that theory. But then that's why she was his ex—he lacked the human compassion she needed, hadn't paid enough attention to her. But how could he? He was too busy keeping these bastards straight, saving the world and all that jazz—taking care of little girls like Darby Shepard.

"We're waiting, Director," Remington reminded him pointedly. "Why is Eve still alive? How did this happen?"

If he were smart, he'd simply blame the decision on Daniel Archer—after all, he was dead. What could they do to him? He certainly couldn't deny the charge. But no, O'Riley wouldn't do that to his old friend. This was his mess; he would clean it up. He'd had his own reasons for making that decision. Reasons they didn't need to know. Daniel Archer had been the one to bring this program to fruition. He deserved better than to be O'Riley's scapegoat.

"The decision was mine," he said bluntly. Looks were exchanged, as he had known there would be, but he ignored the blatant lack of decorum and continued, "She was a ten-year-old child. Our only failure past the sixth division." Not one embryo that had developed past the sixth division had proven to be a failure. Only Eve. "I saw no reason to terminate what I considered an innocent life. Medical wiped her memory and she was entered into the mainstream as an orphaned child with traumatic amnesia."

"Then she had no memory of her time at Center," another member suggested, his tone as well as his expression hopeful.

O'Riley almost laughed at that. Who among these distinguished gentlemen would give the order to terminate Miss Darby Shepard, he wondered? Not a single one. They would leave it up to him—just as they always had.

"I have no reason to doubt Medical's ability to thoroughly cleanse memory imprints," O'Riley agreed. "But that's a chance we can't afford to take."

"Are you suggesting a termination at this late date?" Remington wanted to know.

Ah, a leader with balls. How refreshing, O'Riley mused. Terrence Winslow, the former head of this esteemed group, had certainly possessed none. Then again, this could all be show for the boys around the table.

"A termination may not be necessary," O'Riley offered. "My recommendation would be to send someone in to assess the situation. Someone who could get close to her and determine if she remembers anything about Center. If she understands the true nature of her gift."

"Who would you recommend for the assignment?" This from the newest member of the esteemed group.

O'Riley had already considered who would be the best man for the job. There wasn't even a question. "I've already briefed Aidan. He's ready for the operation."

"Why Aidan?" Remington inquired.

"He's a seer. He'll be able to touch her mind better than any of the other Enforcers." He felt no compunction to go into the other issue. There were things even the Collective didn't need to know. The Enforcers were genetically enhanced creations. As human as O'Riley, only better. They secretly served the world whenever the need arose.

"A seer…" Remington considered the designation for a moment. "In other words, he possesses the same traits that supposedly failed in Eve."

"That's right," O'Riley agreed, though he didn't see the point. The whole frigging room was well aware of what a seer was. "All Enforcers have a heightened ability to read the sensory signals of other humans. Aidan and Eve were the only two we believed to have achieved the highest level of so-called clairvoyance genetically possible. We, of course, later deemed Eve to be a failure. Apparently that was not the case."

"Apparently," Remington parroted.

Another exchange of suspect looks around the conference table. O'Riley really hated this shit. Why didn't they just let him do his job? They'd get their briefing afterwards and his world would be a happy place again.

"Aidan will assess the situation and I will make a decision based on that intel." 'Nough said, O'Riley didn't add.

"When will the Enforcer be ready to move into position?"

"Today." As Center's director, he had never believed in putting off until tomorrow what could be done today. Besides, the situation could blow way out of control in a hell of a hurry. He wasn't completely immune to the urgency or the possible fallout if she suddenly started telling tales outside school, so to speak.

"Is there any chance Galen could connect the woman to us?" the most senior member next to Remington interjected into the conversation.

A kind of hush fell over the room. No one even wanted to think the man's name, much less hear it out loud.

"It's been months since we put him out of business," O'Riley responded. "I don't think we have to worry about him at this point. He lacks the power to strike, even if he were so inclined. There's no reason to believe at this juncture that he has or will make the connection. Eve was a young child when Galen left the program."

"But there is that risk," Remington countered.

"That's right," O'Riley conceded. "There are a number of risks involved. Each is being evaluated and will be handled appropriately."

"Fine." Remington looked around the table. "Any other questions?"

The members of the committee declined further discussion on the matter. O'Riley hadn't expected anything different. None of these men really wanted to know how he planned to handle the situation. They merely wanted it to go away.

So did he.

After the perfunctory handshakes were exchanged, the conference room emptied post haste. Remington loitered at the door, apparently having more on his mind.

"You have another question, Kyle?" O'Riley opened the discussion. No point beating around the bush.

Remington could be president, O'Riley considered with a mental chuckle. He had those all-American boy good looks, even at forty. Blond hair, blue eyes, broad smile that gained him trust and access wherever he needed it. Not for the first time since he'd assumed the leadership of the Collective, O'Riley wondered just what he hoped to do with his future. Whatever his plans, he was keeping quiet about those aspirations at the moment. The Collective was quite happy with President Caroline Winters. Perhaps when her second term was completed, Kyle would make a bid for the White House.

"I just want your personal assurance that this matter is going to go away without trouble. We've scarcely recovered from the whole Winslow-Marsh-Thurlo ordeal. With Galen still at large, I just don't want any more ripples in the stream."

Dr. Waylon Galen was the original creative mind behind the Enforcers. A difference of opinion nearly twenty years ago had formed a division amid the two lead scientific minds developing the project. When the Collective chose Dr. Daniel Archer's assessment over Dr. Galen's, he walked away. He was thought to have died shortly after that. They had since learned that he was not only alive and well, but he'd been plotting for years to overtake what he considered his project once more.

His attempts failed but cost the lives of several people involved with Center, including Dr. Daniel Archer. Though Galen's operation had been disabled, he still represented a threat. One way or another, O'Riley intended to find him. He had no intention of admitting it to Remington but the situation with Darby Shepard had, to his way of thinking, presented an opportunity.

She might be the one final shot he had of luring Galen into a trap.

"You have nothing to worry about, Governor," O'Riley assured Remington. "The situation will be resolved without further incident."

Remington pursed his lips and nodded. "I just need to be sure you've learned something about loose ends in the past sixteen years."

O'Riley's gaze locked with the governor's. "I understand what I have to do, sir. I never make the same mistake twice."

"That's all I needed to hear."

O'Riley watched Remington hurry to catch up with his buddies. He shook his head, a smile tempting his lips. Would wonders never cease? Their new, fearless leader wasn't just putting on the dog for his faithful followers after all. He actually did have the guts to follow through with a suggestion.

Be that as it may, this was still O'Riley's show and he had every intention of doing it his way. Darby Shepard wouldn't be sacrificed until he was certain the elimination was absolutely necessary.

He might be considered a hardcore bastard by most, but he still had a heart.

AIDAN WALKED the dark street, using the night as camouflage for getting the lay of the land. This was his first trip to New Orleans. Though he had studied the necessary maps and cultural background of the city, nothing took the place of firsthand knowledge.

His target had recently changed her place of residence. Apparently her new notoriety came with a price—her privacy. She'd taken a temporary furnished apartment in the Garden District. The school board had insisted she take a leave of absence from her teaching duties until the hoopla surrounding her recent celebrity status died down somewhat. According to Center's intelligence, however, the board intended to let her go permanently. The school was a private institution; the wealthy parents whose children attended didn't want a teacher who possessed such special talents, though it was her special talent that had saved the life of one of those very children.

Darby Shepard—Eve—would have little say in the matter of her future. If his assessment cleared her of being a threat to Center, it would take leaving New Orleans and changing her name for her to get back any semblance of a normal life, he concluded.

He thought about the woman he'd studied on paper before coming here. Her physical features were appealing. Long silky brown hair, pale brown eyes... the color of wet sand. Tall, slender. Yet she looked strong, athletic. Smart, judging by her university scores. But then, why wouldn't she be? Like Aidan, she'd been genetically designed in a lab. Every possible advantage had been assured before the first cell division.

Eve represented the only female Enforcer. Some considered that to be the reason for failure. Perhaps the female of the species just wasn't strong enough for the extent of the gene manipulation to take fully. A remote predisposition for frailty, some theorized. But Aidan didn't think so. He'd watched Eve's history at Center. She'd faked her failure. He was certain of it.

Something about the little girl she had been drew him on an unfamiliar level. He had no real memory of her. It had likely been removed years ago after she was eliminated from the program. But as he'd watched her development from toddler to preadolescent as electronically chronicled by Center, he'd felt a kind of bond with her. They had been educated together, side by side. The only two who possessed the full status of seer. To a degree, they had been separated from the others to protect their elevated ability to read human responses. They had, in effect, been trained and educated in a kind of solitary confinement most of the time. As children, they'd only had each other. Of course, Aidan had been mainstreamed with the others after the age of twelve, when it was deemed he could more readily handle all that he would sense in a multipopulated environment.

Now he and Eve were to be thrown together once more. Only this time, he would be the one judging her true ability. And she would not fool him. He wondered if she ever really had. Perhaps he had known and had simply chosen to keep the information to himself…to protect her.

In any event, things had changed. His assessment would not be influenced by childish delusions.

To a certain degree, she was now the enemy.

He would be her judge and her executioner, if necessary.

When he would have turned the corner from Broadway onto St. Charles, two men stepped out of an alley and blocked his path. The dim glow from the streetlight scarcely offered any real illumination, but his night vision rivaled any technology the military possessed. Light was not required.

"Gimme your wallet, man," the taller of the two growled. He waved the knife in his hand for emphasis.

According to Aidan's research, this area of

the city had a much lower crime rate than certain others. That these men would attempt to mug him surprised him to some degree.

"Is this your usual territory?" he asked the man who'd spoken. Not that it mattered, really; he was merely curious.

"What the hell you talking about? Territory? Just gimme your freakin' wallet!"

"Yeah, man, maybe you don't like your face the way it is," the other one offered as he, too, showed off his weapon of choice.

Aidan frowned. The weapon lacked any length to speak of. Perhaps a four-inch blade. Foolish choice, in his opinion. "Contrary to popular thinking," he said to the second fellow, "size does matter when choosing a weapon."

The taller one lunged for him. Aidan stepped aside in a flash of movement, allowing his adversary to hit the sidewalk face-first. The other made his move then, but he was too slow in addition to lacking a suitable weapon. Aidan grabbed his wrist, twisted viciously, snapping his arm with little effort. The pathetic excuse for a switchblade clinked to the ground seconds before its owner crumpled, howling in pain.

"I'll kill you!"

The first man had regained his footing and was making another dive for Aidan. One swift kick and he was on his knees. A well-placed blow to the back of the head and he wouldn't be getting up again this side of daybreak.

Aidan walked away, leaving the one writhing in agony and the other unconscious.

He decided that the crime statistics of this city couldn't be trusted, which wasn't an actual problem but more of a nuisance.

Continuing along the tree-lined avenue, he watched for the side street that would take him to the eighteenth-century villa-turned-apartment building. The mansion sprawled around a lushly landscaped rear courtyard, which greatly increased its value, according to the real estate information he'd perused on the Internet.

As he approached the building from the rear access, he didn't fear being seen since he wore all black—shoes, slacks, shirt and the full-length duster. He reached into his duster's interior pocket and removed the slide card required to open the electronic lock on the back gate. The technology worked much like the keycards on hotel rooms, only this one was a little more high-tech. Excellent security, unless one gained access to the necessary computer chip. Duplicates could be made of anything if one possessed the right technology. He had not needed to bother with a duplication since he had leased the only vacant apartment.

Inside the enormous courtyard, Aidan paused to survey the area that apparently appealed to the wealthier of the species. Lush plantings, along with a large, ornate fountain, gave the space a tropical feel. Admittedly, the area presented a certain atmosphere of luxury. He turned his attention to the balconies overlooking the courtyard.

Darby Shepard occupied the apartment on the third floor to the left of the building's rear entrance. Despite having moved in only a couple of days ago, a box of blooming flowers tumbled over the lacy ironwork enclosing the balcony. He looked to the empty balcony to the right of hers. That one would lead to his temporary quarters.

He studied the windows on either side of the French doors on her balcony and calculated that the window between their balconies looked directly into her bedroom. She would be sleeping there now. He closed his eyes and cleared his mind, reaching toward her room. Yes, she slept. He sensed no movement of her mind.

In his experience, even his elevated skill didn't allow him to read a person's every thought, especially if they blocked efficiently. He could, however, sense mood and emotion, even intent, quite easily. Thoughts were more difficult. Broadcasting was far easier than reading. She would block him the instant she sensed his awareness level, but he had years of training under his belt that she did not possess.

He would be the stronger one.

Not bothering with the interior stairwell that would lead to their apartments, he scaled the vine-covered trellis. He braced one foot on the edge of his balcony and the other on hers so that he could peer through the window of her bedroom.

To his surprise the window wasn't even closed, much less locked. He pushed the window inward a bit and surveyed her room. The bed stood across the room directly in front of his position. Her hair spilled across the white pillowcase. It looked longer than he'd expected. In the recent photos he'd seen, she'd worn it up in some fashion. But now it was down and splayed over the pillow next to her like a veil of silk. Her long legs looked golden against the white linens that barely draped her body.

Eve was no longer the little girl he remembered. She looked very different...very attractive. His mouth parched as if he'd been many hours without drink. But he had not. This was a physical reaction to her beauty. Just as the hardening sensation in his muscles was. She was beautiful...even more so in repose. An almost overwhelming urge to touch her seared through him. But that would be a mistake.

He watched her a while longer, then climbed onto his balcony and unlocked the French doors the old fashioned way—with a credit card.

Sleep was essential for now. When daylight came, he would make his presence known to her. His profile was simple, a cover she would no doubt trust without second thought.

He did not anticipate that Operation Prophecy would take long. Assessing her skill and memory imprint should be simple. He looked forward to learning about this new Eve.

Aidan stripped off his clothes and climbed into bed.

Sleep came quickly and so did his dreams.

DARBY SAT bolt upright in bed. Her breath rushed in and out in labored gasps. Perspiration beaded on her skin.

Dreaming…she'd only been dreaming.

Of a man. Not the horrible man she'd led the police to, but another stranger.

He'd stood in shadows but she'd felt him watching her. His gaze had moved over her skin like a lover's caress. She shivered even now, wide awake. The darkness had prevented her from making out the details. But she sensed something familiar about him.

But that wasn't possible.

She shivered again and her gaze locked onto the window.

Had she left it open that far?

Rubbing her arms against the sudden chill of the autumn night, Darby climbed out of bed and crossed the room. She peered out over the courtyard that had drawn her to this place. It was so beautiful. She'd always wanted to live in one of these old houses but didn't see the need for the expense. After all, her parents' home sat completely empty.

But everything had changed now.

She doubted it would ever be the same.

The memory of the men in white lab coats made her shiver yet again, and this time she reached for the window's lock. She had to train herself to be more careful now. She had to be aware of her surroundings at all times... aware of those around her at all times.

With a wistful sigh, she turned away from the window and started back toward the bed. She paused midway, her attention inexplicably drawn to the wall that separated her apartment from the neighboring one.

All her senses buzzed to life, drew her to that wall as if it were a flesh magnet.

She moved closer...closer...until she could reach out and touch it. She gasped and drew away, as if the satiny white plaster had somehow burned her. Frowning, she pressed her hand there again, this time without drawing away. A kind of energy flowed through her, excited her on a startlingly primal level. The feeling made her giddy, made her afraid, somehow.

Shaking off the foolish sensations, she climbed back into bed. Too early to start the day yet. With that thought came an uneasy feeling...it followed her back to her dreams.

Chapter Four

"Mr. Yeager, I don't understand why the board is doing this."

Darby's contract had been terminated. This was the reason for Mr. Yeager's call this morning. She'd hoped that he wanted to see her because the board had changed its mind about her continuing to work. But that wasn't the case at all. They wanted her off the school's staff—permanently.

"Ms. Shepard, I know this is difficult." Mr. Yeager had always been kind to her. Despite the pressure she felt sure the board had put on him, he looked sympathetic to her plight. She sincerely regretted that the weariness in his expression was a result of having to deal with her situation.

"Please try and understand the board's position on the matter." He gestured toward the wall of windows across the room. "Look out there. The reporters are circling like vultures. They know you're in here. What kind of environment is that for our children as they come and go to school?"

He was right. She couldn't pretend this away and after three days, it apparently wasn't going away anytime soon. Why couldn't they just leave her alone? She'd told the police all she knew.

Jerry Lester had killed Christina Fairgate. He'd also killed six other children from surrounding communities over the past three years. No one had connected those murders to each other or to him because no bodies had been found. The children were listed as missing. But Lester had a plan. He wanted life in prison, didn't want to face the possibility of a death sentence. He was using the bodies as leverage. Cut him a deal for life rather than death and he'd tell where the bodies were buried.

Darby knew nothing of Lester's work prior to the four New Orleans children who'd gone missing. The media didn't seem to understand that. Those supposedly in the know about clairvoyance called her a liar, claimed she had to know. But she didn't.

Maybe she'd spent so many years block-ing that she couldn't see as much as she needed to. Who was she kidding? She wouldn't have been able to focus her "gift" at all without Madam Talia's assistance. That, thankfully, was still her secret. Madam Talia had told no one.

Oddly, until last night, dreams had not come even without the aid of medication. It was as if Madam Talia had helped her to see what she needed to and the show was over. She saw, felt, nothing else…until last night. A frown nagged at her brow. She'd awoken in the wee hours of the morning in a cold sweat. She'd dreamed of a dark man…touching her… watching her. He had made her feel things she'd never felt before. Her body tingled even now at the memory.

"Don't you agree, Ms. Shepard?"

Darby dragged her attention from the troubling thoughts. "I'm sorry. What were you saying?"

Mr. Yeager looked uncomfortable. He cleared his throat. "You didn't just have one of your visions in my office, did you?" The color drained from his face. "I apologize, Ms. Shepard. I shouldn't have asked that question."

She held up her hand to ward off this new

regret. "No, Mr. Yeager, that's okay. I was just lost in thought, that's all. What were you saying?"

"I thought it would be best if you slipped out the back through the cafeteria while I distract the vultures out front."

Some sense of relief came with that offer, ushering a weary sigh past her lips. "Yes, Mr. Yeager, that would be the best." She stood and reached for his hand. "Thank you, sir, for all you've done. It's been a pleasure working for you. I'll…" She swallowed back the emotion rising in her throat. "I'll clear out my desk and take the personal things from my room later…after some of this has died down."

He shook her hand firmly, placed his other one over their clasped hands. "I truly hate to lose you, Darby. Please take care of yourself and let us hear from you now and again."

She nodded, uncertain of her voice at this point.

Darby didn't miss the sympathetic looks directed her way by the other teachers, but she didn't slow down long enough to talk. She had to hurry. The ladies working diligently to prepare the day's lunch barely noticed her zip through their territory. One or two offered her a grudging smile.

How could saving those children have caused such extreme complications? Instead of being a hero, she was looked at as a freak. Not that she'd done it for any sort of personal gain, certainly not hero status. She'd never wanted to draw attention to herself. But this total shutout was the last thing she'd anticipated. It seemed every friend she'd had was now too busy to even offer condolences for her dire straits. She'd just lost her job, had been forced to move from her home. Even her cat Wiz wouldn't sleep in the bed with her anymore. He preferred the leather sofa in the new place. She was completely alone in this.

As she hurried across the playground at the rear of the school, someone called her name.

Darby turned to find several of the children from her former class racing toward her.

Oh, no.

She should just keep going…shouldn't…

But she just couldn't walk away like that. They wouldn't understand that she was no longer welcome here, that no one wanted her close to their children. Though Anna's parents had been thankful at first, they, too, had feared her continued contact with their child.

It pained Darby deeply. She had no one with whom she could share this hurt, no one to hold her as she cried.

Forcing a smile, she squatted down and offered open arms to the children. They hugged her, a half dozen little voices chiming all at once, asking where she'd been and when was she coming back.

Hard as she tried, she simply could not hold back the tears. She loved these children. This was so unfair.

"I'm afraid I'm going to have to be gone for a while, boys and girls," she said when she recovered her voice. "But you'll have a new teacher and she'll take really good care of you."

"But we want you," little Lisa Andrews said. "We miss you."

"Miss you, too, sweetie." Darby hugged the children closest to her once more. "I'd better be going."

She didn't miss the uncertain looks being cast her way by the other teachers monitoring the playground. They had their jobs to consider, she understood that. It wasn't personal, at least she prayed it wasn't.

Darby stood and waved a final goodbye to the children before striding toward the gate.

She couldn't look back, couldn't bear to see all that she'd worked for slipping away from her.

"Darby!"

As she reached the gate, she turned to face the woman who'd called out to her.

Sandra Paige. Her closest friend at work. The one person she'd expected to be on her side fully in all this. It still stung that she hadn't gotten so much as a call from her friend in the last three days.

Darby bit back the hurt that wanted to well. She would not question her friend. It wouldn't be fair. On some level, she actually understood the reactions she'd encountered.

Sandra hurried to where she stood. Her eyes looked suspiciously bright and Darby had to look away.

"I don't understand why they're doing this," Sandra said, her voice reflecting genuine despair. "I wish there was something I could do."

The words…whispers in her mind…hit Darby with all the force of a hurricane. *No one from this school is to have contact with her. Is that understood?*

Yeager had given that strict order. He, of course, had been ordered to do so by the board. She'd felt his sincerity during their meeting only minutes ago. He hadn't wanted to do this.

"I'm so sorry, Darby."

Sandra hugged her and Darby felt immense relief because now she understood. Her friends hadn't deserted her; they were simply protecting their jobs. She couldn't hold that against any of them.

She drew back and looked into Sandra's eyes. "I'm okay now. Really. I'll be fine. But thank you for offering. That means a great deal to me."

She left, not wanting to risk the media circus out front getting wind of her sneaky departure.

That her friends had not turned their backs on her made the reality of her life at the moment much more tolerable.

She might just get through this after all.

Aidan watched Darby Shepard hurry across the street that flanked the rear of the Iris Goodman School. He didn't have to see her face up close to know that tears spilled down her cheeks. Pain twisted in her chest and she wanted to get away from all of it.

He stayed far enough behind her that she wouldn't feel his presence. Though, he imagined, that if she tried, she would feel him on the other side of the world. Their connection was stronger than he'd expected. He'd felt her reaching for him this morning. Had marveled at the feel of her touching him that way, but he had severed the connection before it went too far. He had to protect his true identity, no matter how tempting her lure.

Darby Shepard knew the back alleys and all the little shortcuts between the school and her new apartment off St. Charles. Aidan considered the trouble he'd run into last night and decided that New Orleans in the daylight was a much less bothersome place.

Just before she moved onto the side street that would lead to the rear courtyard of her building, Darby hesitated, surveyed the pedestrians on the street. Aidan ducked into a doorway a split second before her gaze lit on him. He could feel her searching the crowd. She'd felt his presence. A ghost of a smile tugged at his mouth. She knew he was there on some level, though she might not be certain just yet what the sensations meant.

He would need to be very careful now. She would be cruising for him even when she didn't realize her mind was doing just that. Their bond was too strong to ignore. Even

O'Riley would be startled by the strength of the connection. He had warned Aidan to tread carefully. O'Riley knew more than he was telling. Touching the director's mind was strictly forbidden. Perhaps he should have taken the risk, but his training had long ago become instinct. It was second nature for him to obey the director. But there were things the director didn't have to know. Such as just how close he got to Eve...Darby, he reminded himself.

As long as he didn't blow his cover, he could get as close as he wanted and no one had to know.

All day he'd struggled with the dilemma she represented. Part of him wanted to proceed with caution, but another part of him needed to explore this bond between them. After all these years, how could it still exist? That was the part that baffled him, intrigued him. Sixteen years stood between them. Her memory had been wiped. And yet she still drew him like a moth to the flame. The heat was incredible...burned through him as nothing else ever had. Reason told him it was simply genetic manipulation; they were designed for this bond. But the less rational, more human side of him wondered if part of it could be pure chemistry. A volatile mix just waiting to explode.

He felt her move on. A few moments later, he followed. She hurried across the courtyard and through the rear entrance of the building. Maybe thirty seconds later, she moved onto her balcony, the cordless receiver in hand. He watched until she'd gone back inside, then he crossed the courtyard and entered the building. When he opened the door her cat, Wizard, scampered out without giving Aidan so much as a second look.

He took the stairs two at a time, reaching the third-floor landing in less time than it would have taken to summon the ancient elevator.

Aidan unlocked the door to his apartment and went inside. He moved through the cool, dark interior and paused at the French doors. Opening them wide, he stepped out onto the balcony. He surveyed the grounds, appreciating the fact that the media apparently had not discovered her new place of residence. His next move would be to make her acquaintance. He wondered if she would remember him on some long-buried level. Not likely.

Minutes later, a car sporting a pizza delivery logo pulled up to the back gate. The driver got out and waited to be buzzed in. As Aidan watched, the guy, pizza box in hand, opened the gate and strolled into the courtyard.

A rush of raw energy surged inside him and he knew instantly that it was her. He looked to his left, toward her balcony, just as she breezed through the French doors.

"Up here," she called to the deliveryman. "Take the lift to the third floor. I'll be waiting in the hall. Oh, and let my cat in, would you?"

"No problem," came from the man striding across the courtyard.

Darby suddenly stilled. For three long beats, she didn't move. Slowly she turned her head in Aidan's direction. Their gazes locked. Electricity crackled between them and for a time they could only stare at each other.

"Hey lady! You gonna buzz me into the building or what?"

She blinked, stumbled back a step.

Before Aidan could speak, she'd vanished into her apartment.

Aidan did the same, shedding his leather duster and tossing it onto the sofa as he moved toward the corridor entrance to his apartment. He opened the door and leaned against the frame just to watch her. She paid the pizza guy and he thanked her before heading off.

Her gaze shifted to Aidan and he straightened. "I didn't mean to startle you on the balcony," he said quietly. He moved away from his door, taking a step closer to her. "I'm Aidan." Another step disappeared between them. "Your new neighbor." He thrust out his right hand. "It's a pleasure to meet you."

She was still searching his face, scrutinizing him, when she shifted the pizza to her left hand and placed her right in his. The skin-to-skin contact created a sizzle that made her gasp before she quickly drew back her hand. Startled him just a little as well.

"Darby Shepard. I…didn't know anyone had moved in," she said, her eyes clearly telegraphing her confusion. Her cat strolled up to her door, then wound around her legs before vanishing inside.

"I just moved in last night."

She blinked and thought of how she'd felt his presence this morning. He smiled. Couldn't resist.

"It's quiet around here at night," he noted. "That's good." Considering the rest of the city, it was very good.

She nodded. "Most of the time."

"Well." He glanced at the box in her hand. "I don't want to keep you."

When he would have turned away, she stopped him.

"I'm sorry." She shook her head and laughed softly. "Where are my manners?" She produced a smile in hopes of shielding the awkwardness. It made his heart beat faster. "Please join me. I can't possibly eat all this by myself."

He declined with a wave of his hand. "I wouldn't want to impose."

"No, really." She backed into her apartment to clear him a path. "Come on in."

Aidan closed his own door and moved through hers, ignoring the bombardment of sensations sent his way from merely entering her private residence. He focused on maintaining the mental wall he'd erected. He didn't want her, subconsciously or not, trying to read him.

As she put the pizza box on the table in front of the large overstuffed sofa, she glanced up at him and said, "I just moved in a couple of days ago myself. The apartment belongs to a friend who's living in France for a year. I've been checking on the place for her from time to time. I might as well live here."

She made no mention of her recent troubles, which didn't surprise him. "Your friend has good taste." He walked around the room, assessing the quality of the furnishings and the artwork. "Is this her work?" He studied a vivid piece that reflected the building's courtyard at night.

"Yes." Darby came over to stand beside him. "She's studying art from the masters." She looked up at him, without fear, surprisingly, though he noted the curiosity in her eyes. "Would you like water or a soft drink?"

"Whatever you're having will be fine."

She disappeared into the kitchen, sensing that he was watching her but that didn't stop him. What man wouldn't watch a beautiful woman as she walked away?

When she'd returned with two bottles of cold water and plenty of paper napkins, she was careful to sit opposite him in a chair rather than next to him on the sofa. She passed him a slice of pizza and selected one for herself.

"Are you new to the city?" she asked before taking a bite of the heavily embellished pie.

"Yes," he answered truthfully.

Now she was really curious. He liked that her eyes reflected her every subtle shift in mood. "So what do you think of our wicked city?" Her smile brightened. "We do have a certain reputation, you know."

Aidan found himself returning the smile without conscious effort. It felt strange at first, but not entirely unpleasant. He thought of the two men who'd tried to mug him last night. "The jury's still out on your fair city's reputation."

She laughed. The soft, throaty sound pleased him. He wanted to hear it again.

"I've lived here forever. Any questions you have, feel free to toss them my way." She sipped her water, her gaze never leaving his.

"Forever?" he repeated. "That's a long time, Darby Shepard."

Darby kept her smile in place in spite of the little trickle of uneasiness she felt at the moment. Why had she invited this stranger into her apartment? She'd certainly never done anything like that before. If she'd ever had a reason to be more careful, she had it now. What had she been thinking?

The answer was simple—she hadn't.

She'd been so intrigued by the intensity of the attraction between them that she hadn't given any thought to a single thing, not even her own personal safety.

She'd felt him on that balcony even before she looked his way, just as she'd felt…something…when she woke up in the middle of the night. She'd felt his presence. Not once in her life, that she could recall, had she been so aware of another human being. It thoroughly undid her on one level and drew her on another.

When he'd taken her hand in his to shake it, the sizzle of attraction had been so profound it had stolen her breath. Even now, those dark, dark eyes emanated something… a magnetism she found irresistible. The connection wasn't about how good-looking he was, and he was that. Tall, athletic build. Nice wide shoulders. Long, black hair, almost too long. And the hint of beard— goatee, actually—made him look like a pirate who'd just come ashore. But then when she considered the way he dressed, all in black and with that long duster, his very presence had made her shiver. Had she not seen him standing in the sunlight on that balcony, she'd have sworn he was a vampire straight out of popular fiction.

But he was neither of those things. He was a man, her new neighbor and a mere mortal. Maybe the uproar and uncertainty in her life right now made her want to cling to something solid and strong. If she'd ever laid eyes on a man who looked more solid or strong, she had no memory of the encounter. In fact, Darby felt certain he was like no one else she'd ever met.

"I grew up here," she explained finally, having almost forgotten his question. "My parents—they died in a boating accident a few years ago—loved this city."

"I'm sure you have many happy memories of growing up here," he offered with a smile that took away her breath all over again.

Darby held on to the bottle of water in her hands and tried to think rationally. How could he upset her equilibrium so easily?

"Yes," she replied, though it wasn't completely true. "I have many happy memories. How about you?" She turned the tables, desperate to get out of the spotlight for a while. "Where did you grow up?"

"Out west," he said vaguely. "We moved around a lot."

Something changed in his expression, but she couldn't quite pinpoint the subtle variance. "You have any brothers or sisters?"

He shook his head. "No one. Only me."

Then she understood the change. His parents were gone, too. God, how did she always manage to ask the wrong questions?

"How about more pizza?" she offered in hopes of diverting the sore subject.

"I should go." He pushed to his feet and Darby felt suddenly overwhelmed.

She stood, matching his stance. "I'm glad we could take this opportunity to get acquainted."

That analyzing gaze roved her face, finally settling on her eyes. "Me, too."

Darby followed him to the door, her whole body reacting to the way he moved. There was something incredibly sexy about the way he walked. She shook the silly idea from her head and chastised herself for being so incorrigible.

He hesitated in the open doorway, that fierce gaze latching on to hers once more. "Do you have plans for tonight?"

His voice, more so than the words, made her heart do a little somersault. It was totally irrational. But the deep, soft tones played over her skin, making her shiver, teasing her auditory senses.

Regret lined her face. "I'm sorry. A friend asked me to cover for her on a walking tour at Lafayette tonight." Sudden inspiration struck. "You're new in town, maybe you'd like to come along. We meet at the cemetery gate at nine."

"Sounds interesting," he said noncommittally. "Perhaps I can make it."

"I'll look for you."

Darby closed the door behind him and leaned against it. Very strange. Connecting with him so intensely left her feeling a little out of sorts.

She pushed off the door and banished the unsettling sensations that lingered. She had to figure out what kind of camouflage she would wear tonight. Mary Ellen, her neighbor at her apartment, had taken on an extra flight to Hawaii last weekend and had decided to stay the week. Darby had agreed, before all hell had broken loose, to cover tonight's tour for her. With all that had happened, she'd completely forgotten that it was tonight. It was definitely too late to try to get someone else. She'd just have to figure out a way to prevent being recognized.

If she were really lucky, maybe her handsome new neighbor would show. She could definitely use some more of his attention to boost her waning self-confidence right now. He might be just the distraction she needed to put serial killers and psychic visions out of her mind.

All she wanted was a normal life back.

A good-looking guy was a perfectly normal distraction for an unattached woman her age.

It might as well be Aidan…the mystery man.

Chapter Five

Unspecified Location

"Sir, we have reason to believe there is a connection. According to my intelligence, Center has sent an Enforcer to New Orleans."

Waylon Galen shook his head. "That's impossible. She was eliminated. A failure." Center's only failure, but a failure nonetheless. He refused to believe that Marsh had misled him. Joseph Marsh had worked at Center, been involved at the deepest level. He would have known this. Hell, even Archer's own files had indicated the elimination. *This* had to be a mistake.

"Sir," the only human being Galen trusted at the moment continued, "I believe the situation merits further investigation."

Galen had lost everything. His covert position within the Colombian government's realm. His lab. His only reliable contacts within the U.S. government. And none of that was nearly so important as his connection to Center. Winslow had been his last contact with the work that was his.

He created the Enforcers!

Galen pushed to his feet, sending his chair banging against the credenza.

He was the one who started it all. And they took that away from him. Forced him out. Then left him to languish on his own. But he'd come back. Determination surged through him. He'd almost reached that pinnacle of mastery yet again. Only to be thwarted by the likes of O'Riley.

Now, just maybe, he had one last chance.

If Eve still existed, if the woman in New Orleans was really the seer he himself had created, he still had a foot in the door.

"I'll need to look into this personally," he said to his intelligence analyst.

"Sir, are you sure that's a good idea? They'll be on the lookout for you." He shoved the thick glasses up the bridge of his nose. "It could be a trap. Perhaps they want us to believe it's her so they can lure you there."

Perhaps. That was a chance he'd simply have to take.

"Make the arrangements," Galen ordered. "I'm leaving immediately."

His analyst nodded. "Yes, sir."

"Oh, and Brewer."

Tad Brewer, his confidant and senior analyst, hesitated at the door. "Sir?"

"I'm very impressed with your work. I won't forget how reliable you've been."

Brewer nodded and rushed off to do his superior's bidding.

Galen laughed softly. O'Riley thought he had everything under control. He just didn't know how far a desperate man could go. When he realized his miscalculation, it would be far too late.

New Orleans
City of the Dead

SOMEONE WAS following her.

She'd felt it all through the tour.

Had felt someone watching her too closely. Not like the tourists who'd paid for the opportunity to traipse through one of New Orleans' most famous cemeteries.

This had been different and wholly focused on her.

Darby watched the last of the tourists disappear through the massive, yawning gates. One more tour was scheduled later tonight, and then the cemetery would be closed and locked up tight. Thankfully, she wasn't the guide for that midnight tour.

Shivering she rubbed her arms. October was the second-largest tourist season in New Orleans. All month long, special "terrorizing" tours were offered. Costume parties went on at local bars and clubs every weekend, sometimes even on weeknights.

The distant sounds of laughter and jazz floated on the autumn night's breeze. New Orleans never slept. There was always a party, always music, always people. Some streets never completely cleared.

Time to get out of here, she reminded herself as another shudder rippled through her. She wasn't really afraid of her hometown in the dark. She'd grown up here, knew the streets that were safe and the ones to avoid. Her bicycle was parked on the grounds. She'd be home in no time.

The moon hung low and big tonight. Something else to be thankful for, she mused, as she moved through the cemetery toward the Shriner's Tomb where she'd parked her bike. She'd played near that big old tomb as a child. Whenever she came here, that was always where she ended up.

A frown tugged the corners of her mouth downward as the fog seemed to thicken and swirl around her feet. Had Benny, the guy in charge of special effects, forgotten to turn off the machine that produced that eerie stuff whenever nature didn't comply? She didn't remember it being so thick an hour ago. She supposed it didn't matter. It was 10:30. The next tour started at midnight. Someone would shut it off. She had no idea where he positioned the machine, or even how it worked, or if—really big if—it was even providing this lovely, deepening element of graveyard atmosphere.

The fine hairs on the back of her neck stood on end once more as the undeniable sensation that she was being watched slid down her spine a second time tonight. She refused to look around like a fraidy cat. There was no one here. She was fine. Her only enemy was locked up tight in a New Orleans jail.

The aboveground tombs rose upward out

of the fog like ghostly white temples. A cluster of clouds floated past the moon, casting darker-than-death shadows and adding yet another layer of uneasiness to her mounting anxiety. She was really letting this get to her.

She hastened her step, refusing to outright run, moving quickly past praying angels and marble crosses, through the now murky moonlight scarcely piercing the shadows cast by moss-laden oaks. All she had to do was get on her bike and pedal home. She'd be there in no time.

Stumbling in her haste, Darby barely caught herself before she fell. She tried to slow her racing heart, cast around quickly to regain her bearings. She knew this cemetery. That's why she'd agreed so readily to do the tour for her friend. She knew as much or more about this place than most of the tour guides being paid for their services. This was pure foolishness.

She sucked in a bolstering breath and silently thanked God when the clouds moved away from the full moon. Forcing her gaze forward, she started toward her destination once more. She ignored the crumbling headstones that usually garnered her attention. Refused to even glance at the marble guard dogs that now seemed to growl silently at her. Even the gargoyles sitting atop the next tomb she passed appeared to sneer down at her.

The second she reached her bike, she released the lock that held it immobile, dropped it into her purse and swung her right leg over the seat. Time to get home. She'd seriously let the night creeps get to her. Something she hadn't done since…she couldn't even remember when.

She pedaled through the swirling fog, keeping her gaze focused straight ahead. All she had to do was head toward the sound of music, toward the laughter of revelers.

Swearing hotly, she braked to a stop outside the gate. She had to close the gates. Dammit. She'd almost forgotten. Darby shoved the kickstand down and left her bike long enough to drag one massive gate at a time to the neutral position. Though she didn't have the key to lock it, closing it, according to her friend, was a precaution to keep honest folks honest. The next guide would lock the gates for the night after the final tour.

"Looks like I'm a little late."

A shriek escaped her before she could pre-

vent it. She spun around to find Aidan waiting near her bike.

"Lord, you scared me half to death." Not
that it had taken much. She pressed her hand
to her chest and ordered her thundering heart
to slow. Two deep breaths later and she felt
a little more in control.

"I'm sorry," he offered, moving closer.

It wasn't until he stepped from beneath the
canopy of the trees that she really got a good
look at him. Dressed all in black as he was,
about the only thing that stood out were those
eyes. As dark as they were, there was a kind
of light that emanated from them, a beacon
that drew her.

His extraordinary good looks devastated
her all over again. She'd known handsome
men before. Certainly in a city this large, a
girl ran into a good-looking man now and
then. But this went well beyond the usual
meaning of the word. His male beauty was
entirely compelling…in a dangerous sort of
way. She shivered.

Even the overlong hair she didn't usually
care for looked good on him. It curled around
the collar of his shirt. Blue-black silk against
the denser black of his shirt. The goatee that
framed his mouth did nothing to distract

from the sculpted lips that did strange things to her tummy. Made her yearn to know how the man kissed.

And she'd only just met him today.

Okay. Reality check here. Apparently dreaming about serial killers and men in little white coats had pushed her over the edge of reason. Certainly all good sense she'd ever possessed was long gone. Made the dreams about the men in the little white coats actually prophetic. They might just show up to take her away any time now.

"You...missed the...tour," she stammered, completely at a loss as to what else to say.

"It appears so." He moved a step closer. "Unless you'd like to give me a personal tour."

It was the long duster he wore, she decided then and there. Not much imagination was required to go from that to a long, black cape. Oh, yeah, her new neighbor could be one of those seductive vampires in the latest popular fiction novel. She should be afraid. She should be very afraid.

"There's no need to be afraid," he said softly, reading her mind. "It's just a cemetery, right?"

There was something about the way he

spoke, or maybe it was the way he took her arm and wrapped it around his before entering the gates of her favorite city of the dead. Whatever it was, she found it stirring, mesmerizing. She simply couldn't resist. If he wanted a tour…he would get a tour.

He walked through the ankle-deep mist beside her, his movements sleek, confident, as smooth as glass. How could a man with such a hard-muscled physique move so fluidly? So effortlessly?

Aidan couldn't take his eyes off her.

She was beautiful. Even more so with her face caressed by moonlight. Moonlight that played with shadow, always moving, never constant, giving her ethereal beauty an even more haunting glow. The smell of her skin…the softness of it tempted him beyond reason.

He hadn't made his presence known earlier because he hadn't wanted to be distracted the way he was now. He'd needed to be on guard while the crowd surrounded her. But now, it was only the two of them. He could relax. Relax and enjoy being near her. There was something so sensual about her innocence, her utter humanness. He'd spent his entire life with those genetically superior—

she was genetically superior—and yet she emoted a vulnerability, fragility, a neediness he had never known.

She drew the gauzy black scarf from her hair, allowing it to fall loose. "My disguise," she said with a laugh and tucked the scarf into her pocket.

The cool breeze stirred her long hair, lifting it, playing with it momentarily and then allowing it to drape over her shoulders and down her back like a cape of shiny silk. Her eyes captured the sparse light from the moon and glowed softly with it. No one else at Center had eyes like hers.

He forced himself to focus on the musical sound of her voice as she related the history behind each headstone. He did so enjoy listening to her talk. It made him feel as if he'd come home...reached some place that he was meant to be. This bond they'd shared as children was damn strong. Stronger than even he'd realized until this moment.

"They've filmed movies here," she was saying. "You've probably seen at least one."

"Probably," he agreed, smiling to himself.

She glanced up at him and returned his smile. "Why are you looking at me that way?"

He looked past the glimmer of uncertainty

in her eyes and read the genuine curiosity. She wanted to understand this connection as well. She felt it, not quite so strongly as him, however.

"It's difficult not to look at one so beautiful," he said in all honesty. "I'll try to resist the temptation."

She laughed that pleasant sound that made him want to taste her lips to see if they tasted as good as they looked and sounded. Unexpected—everything about her was unexpected.

"If you're trying to seduce me, Aidan, it's working a little too well." She stopped and looked into his eyes. "We just met," she said carefully. "This is moving a little too fast for me."

"Then we'll slow things down." His gaze dropped to her mouth and it took all the willpower he possessed not to kiss her. Her mouth looked full and soft, the bottom lip heavier, poutier. "You set the pace, Darby Shepard."

She nodded, her gaze now focused on his lips. She wanted to kiss him as well. He could feel her desire, could feel her heated blood coursing through her veins. She wanted more than just to kiss him.

A new kind of tension quickened inside

him. A warning. His head came up and his gaze narrowed as he surveyed the ancient cemetery. He felt another's presence…felt him watching. He was not so close, but close enough.

"Maybe we can finish this tour another time. It's late." He infused the offer with a smile. "I'll walk you home."

She nodded, the confusion in her eyes telling him that she'd felt the shift in the atmosphere as well. Felt the presence of the enemy without comprehending the full implications.

She might not have honed her skills as he had over the past sixteen years, but she was undeniably a seer.

When the gates were closed once more, Darby pushed her bike as she walked alongside Aidan. For the third time tonight, she felt someone watching her. Funny she hadn't sensed Aidan's presence until he was only a few feet away. Though she supposed it could have been him she felt watching her as she closed up after the tour, she didn't think so. Some part of her recognized him on a very basic level. The other presence had been unfamiliar…unsettling… like the one she was picking up on right now.

With Aidan at her side, she wasn't actually

afraid. She felt secure with him. Still, she didn't like this feeling of being watched. She wondered somewhere in the back of her mind if the police had someone watching her. Maybe she would call Detective Willis and ask that very question.

As they left the cemetery behind, the din of Friday night revelers in the distance grew louder. Jazz moaned woefully from a club just one street over. A few blocks away, strip bars and clubs hosting costume parties would be in full swing. The crowd on the sidewalk and in the streets grew thicker and rowdier. This was part of what she loved about New Orleans. It was a city full of life. Even the dead seemed to generate some sort of energy.

She suddenly realized that she hadn't even thought of Lester. The images she'd kept seeing were gone. Maybe it was over. Though she felt terrible for the parents of those children whose bodies were still missing, at least their killer was behind bars and would be punished for his terrible sins.

His reign of terror was over. She'd helped to end it. The price had been high, but she would do it again if only to save a single child.

When they reached the gate to the courtyard of the place she currently called home, Aidan used his keycard and opened it for her. He'd offered to push her bike but she preferred to do it herself. It gave her something to do with her hands, rather than the carnal thoughts her mind had conjured. She kept wondering what it would be like to run her fingers through his hair or to touch his chest. Or those mile wide shoulders.

She sighed. The man was simply every woman's fantasy wrapped in sleek black.

The sensation of being watched had melted blocks ago, or maybe the heat he emanated had distracted her. Whatever the case, she was glad she no longer had that icky feeling. She parked her bike in an out-of-the-way corner of the lobby and locked it. No need to lug it up to the third floor.

He followed her into the lift and closed the gate that served as a door. She pressed the button for Floor Three and the rickety old elevator shuddered into movement. Her companion chose to lean against the wall farthest from her so that he could stare at her, apparently. She crossed her arms over her chest and surveyed the ancient elevator. It was nothing fancy, but she appreciated its antiquity. Except tonight her preoccupation was to keep her eyes busy…and off the man who did strange things to her sensibilities.

"My admiration disturbs you?" he inquired, seemingly sincere.

She chewed her lower lip and tried to think of a witty comeback. "Well, disturb isn't quite the word. It makes me uncomfortable."

He shifted his gaze immediately. "I'll remember that."

She shook her head and tried to find logic in this crazy attraction. How could he come out of nowhere and sweep her off her feet so completely?

She didn't even know him.

She exhaled a tension-filled breath. But Lord have mercy, she was attracted to him.

At her door he hesitated. "Good night, Darby Shepard," he said softly, his gaze once again falling on hers.

"Good night, Aidan…?" She lifted a skeptical brow. "I don't even know your last name."

"Tanner," he told her. "Aidan Tanner."

She reached for his hand and shook it. "Well, good night, Aidan Tanner."

His fingers closed firmly around her hand as he lifted it to his mouth and brushed the barest hint of a kiss across her knuckles. "Until tomorrow."

And then he was gone.

His apartment door closed behind him.

Darby was still trying to get her heart out of her throat when she locked her own door behind her. This just couldn't be real. No way could *he* be real.

She stripped off her clothes as she headed toward her bathroom. Guys like him just didn't exist. She pushed the drain plug into place and turned the water in the big old claw-footed tub to hot. A long, hot bath was in order.

The few minutes she took to scrub her face clean and to floss and brush her teeth was all the time required for the tub to fill. She added a couple of drops of rose oil and gathered two big, fluffy towels. Every woman deserved this kind of bath after a long day. She couldn't help wishing she had a tub like this back at her apartment.

It might not be a whirlpool, but it was so deep that the water enveloped her clear up to her neck. The heat permeated her, immediately driving away the tension, forcing her muscles to relax.

"God, this feels good," she murmured.

She closed her eyes and leaned back, relaxing fully. Without an exhaust fan, the bathroom filled with steam, making it as foggy as the cemetery had been tonight.

Thinking of the cemetery made her think of Aidan.

Now whenever she thought of him, she would immediately associate him with heat and silk, shadows and fog. Her feminine muscles pulsed, flexing and contracting with want. The man completely devastated her…on far too many levels. He made her hot just looking at him. And the sound of his voice…how could any man's voice flow so slow and deep, sliding over her skin like warm honey?

Her nipples pebbled and her breasts hardened, ached for his touch. Hmmm. She smiled and imagined those long fingers stroking her skin. Heat swirled deep inside her.

The water felt so good, so welcoming.

She didn't want to move, just wanted to keep thinking of him…of how it would feel to have him in this massive tub with her. A new kind of awareness went through her at the remembered feel of his lips on her skin when he'd kissed her hand.

Her mind conjured the image of him coming toward her, through the mist and steam rising around her. He slipped beneath the water, his hot, smooth flesh sliding against hers, creating a sensual friction that made her pulse leap and her heart pound. He was against her and all around her at once, shrouding her like steel encased in silk. Music, so soft it could have come from within her—the beat could have been her pulse—swirled around her, filled her. She felt his lips on her heated skin. She gasped, clutched at the sides of the tub as those hungry lips moved down her body, tantalizing her flesh. Her name whispered through her mind...the sound his voice. The touch all around her...his touch. Tighter and tighter, desire coiled inside her. Her breath grew ragged and her hips writhed beneath the water, beneath the weight of his presence.

She came. It pulsed deep inside her, throbbed through her soul and wrenched a cry from her throat.

For long minutes, she couldn't move, couldn't open her eyes. She could only lie there, sated and utterly vulnerable.

Slowly she became aware of a change, a shift in the atmosphere of the room.

His essence was gone.

She opened her eyes and the spell was broken.

The water that had felt so hot a second ago was cold, making her shiver uncontrollably. The steam and mist that had filled the room had dissipated.

She watched a bead of moisture slide down the mirror as her heart rate returned to normal.

It had felt so real…as if he'd been right here with her.

She pushed up out of the cold water and shook off the crazy notion.

Just a dream.

She'd likely drifted off to sleep and dreamed of him. He'd been on her mind, had gotten her all hot and bothered tonight. That's all it could be.

As the tub drained, she dried her hair and skin, all the while chastising herself for getting so hung up on her new neighbor. A distraction was one thing, but this fantasizing went way beyond a mere distraction.

Not bothering to dry her hair, she wrapped a towel around it and wandered into her bedroom. She was beat. She'd deal with bed head in the morning.

As she drew the covers back she couldn't

help thinking of her neighbor just on the other side of that wall. Before she could stop herself, she'd walked over to the wall that stood between them and placed her hand there. Just like last night, it felt hot to the touch. She frowned, shook her head and touched it again. Cool plaster greeted her this time.

Her imagination, she assured herself. She had to get this silly infatuation out of her head.

Aidan was just a guy.

A handsome one, admittedly, but just a guy.

She had enough troubles right now without borrowing more.

Tomorrow, she would begin the search for a new job. She couldn't stay unemployed forever. Though she had fair-sized savings and her parents' home, that was no excuse to sit around and feel sorry for herself.

Work. She needed work.

Clearly a distraction with her new neighbor wasn't the proper therapy for her just now.

No matter how right it felt.

Chapter Six

"Ms. Shepard, your résumé looks excellent."

Darby held her breath. Please let him say yes.

The administrator for the Riverwalk Preschool looked at her over his wire-rimmed glasses. "I appreciate your candor regarding your current dilemma with the media. I am quite aware of the circumstances."

The air evacuated her lungs on a weary sigh. Here it came. The kiss of death. She was qualified—overqualified—but the preschool simply wouldn't be able to tolerate the negative notoriety.

"I see no reason why such unfair circumstances should keep a good teacher out of work."

Relief, so profound it made her feel momentarily faint, rushed through her veins. She had a job!

"Thank you, Mr. Wesley. I really love working with children."

He smiled. "I can see that." He glanced at his watch. "It's almost noon and our small Saturday group will be leaving. How about you begin Monday morning. Eight o'clock?"

She nodded. "That's perfect." She stood and offered her hand. "Thank you so much, Mr. Wesley. I appreciate your confidence."

"I'll give you a quick tour of our facility on your way out," he offered.

Most of the children were gone already, but Darby got to meet two that would be in her weekday class. The preschool offered preparatory classes Monday through Friday, from 7:30 until 3:30. An evening day care continued from three until six. Then on Saturdays, from nine until noon, a mothers' morning out drop-off was offered for those who couldn't manage to shop and keep up with kids at the same time.

The atmosphere was very inviting, family-oriented. Darby felt comfortable immediately. She met three other teachers who, like her, had a primary education degree. Every instinct told her that this would be a perfect fit. The preschool was close enough to home that she could ride her bike or the streetcar.

Its focus was on preparing the children for elementary school.

It was perfect.

Darby left the preschool and walked along Canal Street. She hadn't bothered with her bike since it was such a lovely morning. The air had been fresh and crisp. Even now, at quarter of twelve, it wasn't too warm.

She surveyed the busy sidewalks filled with tourists and shoppers. The buzz of excitement that defined New Orleans felt thick in the air. Jazz notes wafted from the horn of a lone sax player hoping to make a few bucks on a street corner this morning. Darby paused and tossed a dollar into the open instrument case at his feet. He nodded, never missing a note, and she smiled, grateful for the day…for her new job.

And for her new temporary neighbor.

She gave herself a little mental shake as she continued to meander through the crowd. She hadn't seen him this morning. His presence, though, had been palpable. He was at home, she'd felt certain. Maybe still sleeping when she left for her interview at 10:30, though she didn't take him for one to waste such a beautiful day in bed. Unless he had the proper motivation. Instantly, the image of the two of them naked and in his bed flashed in her mind.

Okay, Darby, focus. The man was not some sex object whose sole purpose was to fuel her fantasies. Nor was he a stray puppy to be cuddled and taken in without question. Especially considering what she'd just been through with a killer. She, of all people, knew what man was capable of.

That she felt no fear of Aidan Tanner unsettled her.

Not that she generally walked around suspicious, but she'd always been cautious. Her parents had raised her to be smart and level-headed when it came to men and life in general. Sometimes she wondered if her cautious nature had something to do with the dreams about the men in white coats.

A chill raced across her skin even as she allowed the thought. Her parents had adopted her when she was ten, but her memories prior to that were sketchy at best. She vaguely remembered school…somewhere. Hard as she tried, she couldn't dredge up any recollection of her biological parents, though she'd seen pictures of them. There was a close bond of some sort from that time. She remembered it…still sensed it. With her parents, she presumed. The lingering memory of that connection made her feel safe sometimes in the middle of the night when she felt all alone.

She missed the Shepards. They'd been such good people, had loved her as their own. She wondered why it wasn't the bond she'd experienced with them that made her feel safe in moments of personal indecision or crisis. Why some almost forgotten connection with a person or persons she didn't even remember?

Darby suddenly stopped in the middle of the block and looked around. She blinked, utterly surprised, then smiled. She was out in public and no one had approached. No cameras were snapping away, no dogged reporters were following her. Could it possibly be over?

She looked heavenward then and thanked God for yet another blessing.

Maybe she really would get her life back now.

Not willing to take any unnecessary chances on being spotted by any loitering paparazzi, Darby took a side street that was a bit off the beaten path. She ignored the couple arguing in a doorway as she passed. Paid no attention to what looked like a gang hanging out on the corner with a boom box blaring the latest rap chart hit.

This was New Orleans. Nothing was out of place; nothing surprised longtime residents. She just kept marching forward, head held high, shoulders squared, showing no fear. This was her home, same as for those who loved to intimidate. Catcalls and whistles echoed behind her as she moved past the gang of what her mother would have called thugs. Probably just young guys with nothing else to do.

She crossed the street to the next block which was tree-lined to the point of near darkness. She refused to allow the uneasiness to take root as she pushed forward, moving out of the warm sunlight and into the ominous shadows. Ancient houses sat so close together that hardly a sprig of grass separated them. Each had its own little postage-stamp front yard that consisted mainly of huge old oak trees which canopied the sidewalk and street like a protective awning.

Only another block or so and she'd hit St. Charles and the generous sunlight the October sky offered. As she passed an alley between two shops, someone called her name. She hesitated, frowned. At least she thought she'd heard her name called. Maybe it was her imagination. She stepped closer to the alley and peered into the dark passage. A Dumpster. Garbage cans. Not much else. A cat hissed and jumped down from an open can, leaving whatever treasures it contained to two other, more aggressive felines sitting atop it, tails twitching.

Darby Shepard. The whispered words feathered across her nerve endings, making her shiver.

She moved closer still, cocking her head, listening, watching, for any sound...any movement.

"Madam Talia sent me."

Darby drew up short, gasping for the oxygen currently evacuating her lungs.

"Shhh!" the woman warned.

Darby reclaimed her composure and moved farther into the deep shadows. "Who are you?" Fear should have skittered up her spine, but it didn't.

"I work for Madam Talia. She sent me here to give you a message."

Darby almost laughed. How could Madam Talia have known that she would take this route? She hadn't even known.

"What kind of message?" Darby's eyes

had adjusted to the lack of light and she could see that it was, indeed, the receptionist from Madam Talia's place of business. "How did you know I'd be here?"

The woman smiled. She was much shorter than Darby and a bit on the heavy side. Forty-five or fifty, maybe. Her smile warmed her usual, business-like expression.

"Madam Talia knows many things, Ms. Shepard," she reminded.

Darby nodded. She definitely couldn't deny the assertion. She sensed that Madam Talia was a very powerful woman. The only question in her mind was the source of that power.

"She wanted me to warn you that your life is in grave danger."

If she'd said most anything else, Darby wouldn't have been surprised. But this...the nightmares were over. Lester was in jail awaiting trial or arraignment...whatever.

"How? From who? I don't understand," she said, shaking her head. "Lester is in jail. He can't hurt me—"

The woman manacled her arm. "Listen to her!" she whispered harshly. "She never makes a mistake."

For the first time since she heard her name

called, she felt a prick of fear. "Surely she gave you some idea of how my life was in danger."

This didn't make sense. Why wouldn't she sense the danger herself? The only change in her life was the whole business with helping those kids and putting Lester behind bars. Well, she amended, there was a new job and Aidan. Surely he meant her no harm. He'd certainly had the perfect opportunity last night to hurt her if that were his intent.

"This doesn't make sense," she murmured aloud before the woman could answer her question.

"Madam Talia said to tell you that the threat comes from the men in the white coats. She said you would understand."

Ice-cold terror slid through Darby's veins. "You're certain that's what she said?"

The woman nodded gravely.

"Thank you," Darby managed, the words brittle. "Thank Madam Talia. I…" Her voice betrayed her, quavering with fear. "I have to go."

She turned away, her movements stiff, awkward.

"Better lock your door," the woman called after her.

Darby stalled just beyond the mouth of the alley, her feet mired in the sidewalk that suddenly turned to swampy quicksand.

One, two, I'm coming for you. Three, four, better lock your door.

Time lapsed into slow motion. Silence coagulated around her. Darby turned, the movement seeming to take an eternity. Her gaze went back to the dark alley and the woman who'd delivered the warning.

She was gone.

Darby blinked, and time and place zoomed back into vivid focus. She spun slowly around amid the chaos that was constant, an everyday part of New Orleans life. The chaos that had been strangely missing only moments ago when she had been alone in an alley with the woman Madam Talia had sent. The sunlight reached through the trees and warmed her face. The music from the boom box blasted her eardrums. The guys loitering on the corner of the last block danced, blatantly sexual moves to the erotic beat. And the couple in the doorway was lost in a passionate kiss.

The threat comes from the men in the white coats.

They knew she was here.

The realization shook her like the propulsion from a rocket during takeoff.

In that instant, a new awareness settled deep into her bones.

They were coming for her.

WHEN SHE'D REACHED the gate to the courtyard behind her apartment, Darby paused to catch her breath. She glanced warily, first right and then left. The side street was empty. No one had followed her and yet every step of the way she'd felt as if someone was right on her heels.

Maybe the warning had merely made her paranoid. Whatever the case, she couldn't shake the overwhelming sense that more than one set of eyes watched her.

She rested her forehead against the wrought-iron gate and released a heavy breath. She hated this feeling. Hated when things spun out of control. It hadn't happened often in her life…well, at least during the parts that she remembered clearly.

When she'd first come to live with the people she would eventually learn to love and call Mom and Dad, she'd felt completely out of control. That time in junior high when she'd let the visions overtake her life. Then again when she'd lost her parents in that boating accident. Those were the only times she could remember this gut-wrenching sense of dread… of imminent disaster.

She slid her keycard in the lock and entered the courtyard. The fear was the worst part. She hated being afraid. Though she'd always worried that the men in the white coats would come for her if she wasn't careful, she'd never really been afraid. She'd convinced herself that it was all a bad dream. Leftover anxieties from whatever life she'd lived before.

But now it felt entirely too real.

Madam Talia wouldn't have warned her otherwise. The woman hadn't garnered her impeccable reputation by tossing around groundless accusations and empty warnings. Darby had to face the fact that her past was after her. Instinct and plain old common sense told her that it had something to do with her name and face being splashed all over the papers.

Somehow, her so-called heroism had alerted whomever the men in the white coats represented. The way she saw it, she had two options here. She could sit back and wait for them to come, or she could start digging and see what she found.

When facing an enemy of any sort, it was always best to be prepared.

"Am I too late to offer to take you out to lunch?"

Aidan was propped against the wall outside her apartment door when she reached her floor. Her smile was automatic. How could she not smile with a guy like that looking at her as if she were everything he'd ever wanted? For lunch and otherwise.

The connection was immediate and intense. This couldn't be mere chemistry. It was far too strong. She shivered with acute awareness.

"No," she replied. "You're definitely not too late." She gestured to her door. "Would you like to come in? I need to check my messages and let Wiz out."

Taking his time, he surveyed her from head to toe. His gaze was like a slow, gentle caress. "I can't believe such a beautiful lady would go shopping and come back empty-handed. Didn't they have anything you desired?"

She clamped down on her lower lip a moment to stop its silly quivering. Lord, maybe lunch wasn't such a good idea. Some wanton female side she hadn't known existed took over whenever he was near. "I didn't go shopping," she confessed. "I had a job interview."

His expression turned to one of understanding. "I see."

Before she could think what to say next he took the key from her hand and slid it into the slot and opened her door. "I'll just be across the hall. Let me know when you're ready to go." He offered the keycard back to her.

"It's okay." She accepted the keycard and dropped it into her purse. She had to stop running so hot and cold, had to find some neutral spot. "Come on in. I won't be long." She cooed a greeting to Wiz and promised him a trip outside.

Whether the distraction her neighbor posed was smart right now or not, she needed to keep her mind off that warning, away from the fear. She had to think, prepare some game plan. There had to be a way to dig into her past and find the answers she needed.

She thought about the self-hypnosis she'd studied, wondered if that might work. She might need help for that. Could she still call upon Sandra? Her gaze settled on her handsome neighbor. Did she dare trust him with that kind of personal information?

He was busy studying a picture a parent of one of her students had taken of her last Christmas. In the photo, she was surrounded by her students, all dressed as angels for the Christmas play. She'd brought a few mementoes with her to make the place feel more like home. Sadness welled in her chest. She did so miss the children. It would take a while for her to fit in at the new job, but she would never forget the wonderful memories she'd made at her old school.

Pushing the sentimental thoughts away, she dropped her purse on the sofa and depressed the Play button for the telephone answering machine on the table by the sofa. Maybe Mary Ellen had called from Hawaii to check on how the tour had gone.

There was only one message.

The male voice echoed in the room. "Ms. Shepard, this is Detective Willis. I've been trying to contact you all morning. I've called several times and there has been no answer. One of my men has been by your apartment as well. The landlord allowed him inside to ensure that you weren't injured and in need of assistance."

Darby took an unsteady step back from the machine as if the words threatened her somehow. She sensed the danger. Aidan was suddenly at her side but she couldn't find her voice—couldn't say anything. She could only stare into his eyes and listen as Detective Willis continued.

"The moment you get this message, assuming one of my men doesn't find you first, please call me. It's imperative. Jerry Lester has escaped. You may be in danger. Please call me, Ms. Shepard."

A beep sounded and the tape machine shut off.

For a full minute, Darby just stood there, staring at it, not certain what she should do next. Lester was out; he knew what she'd done.

He knew who she was.

The pounding on her door broke the tension. She jerked at the sound.

Before she could react, Aidan had gone to the door and peered through the peephole. "It's a police officer," he told her quietly.

She crossed to the door and he stepped aside, moved to the other side of the room, giving her space. Steeling herself, she took a deep breath and opened it.

"Ms. Shepard, I'm Officer Dennehy. Detective Willis asked me to keep an eye on your apartment. I just wanted you to know that me and my partner will be right outside the building if you need us."

She nodded. "I just got home," she said brokenly.

"We know, ma'am. Please keep your door locked and you'll need to call Detective Willis. We've already let him know you're here."

She nodded again. "Thank you."

Aidan remained silent while Darby did as the officer instructed. She closed and locked the door, then made the call to Willis.

This was an unforeseen complication. Center would need to be made aware before the news hit the general public. O'Riley did not like being blindsided. The killer's escape guaranteed more media coverage and increased the likelihood of Galen's discovering Eve's existence.

He'd watched her all morning, had noted the covert meeting with the woman in the alley. Her warning had been whispered, but even whispered and from a half a block away—if he focused—his auditory senses picked up enough of the conversation to piece together the threat.

Men in white coats.

Aidan had an uneasy feeling that meant only one thing—Center. It was the first indication he'd had that Darby remembered anything, but that in itself was not enough to form an accurate conclusion. He needed more intel.

She moved to the French doors and stared toward the courtyard. Her inner turmoil reached out to him. She felt frightened on one level but furious on another. Oddly, he didn't think the escaped killer worried her as much as the warning the woman in the alley had issued.

He supposed the danger she knew and understood felt far less threatening than the one she didn't.

He admired her beauty once more as the sun kissed her cheek, brought out the gold highlights in her long brown hair. Even dressed in a conservative jumper that fell just shy of her ankles, she appealed to him on a physical level. The slit in the jumper had revealed a satiny length of thigh with each step she'd taken as she'd walked this morning. A simple white blouse, sleeveless and scoop-necked, hugged her upper torso beneath the pale green jumper. The delicate sandals on her feet looked immensely feminine, but it was the pink toenails that disturbed him the most.

"Are you all right?" he asked softly as he approached her.

She trusted him; he'd felt her responding to him from the beginning. Last night had proven his assessment. He thought of the way his mind had so easily touched hers. He could taste her even now. He thought again of the way her skin smelled...the softness of it. He wanted to touch her now...not like last night. For real this time.

Not yet...it was too soon.

She'd been brought up amid humans who reveled in fantasy but faltered in reality. She could, in effect, enjoy the fantasy without fear of repercussion. And yet she had no idea just how real this fantasy was.

"I'm okay."

He moved closer still. "I won't let him hurt you," he promised, knowing an explanation would be in order. But it was time he moved this operation to the next level.

That gaze, the color of glittering sand after the tide rolled back from the shore, collided with his. "Thank you for offering, but I couldn't drag you into this."

He couldn't resist. He had to touch her. He

reached up slowly, so as not to frighten her, and pushed aside a lock of silky hair from her cheek.

"I'm already a part of it."

Confusion claimed her expression. "I'm not sure I understand what you mean."

He took her small hand in his, closed his fingers around its softness. The energy that hummed between them pumped up a notch. She felt it; her pulse reacted. Her heart began to pound.

"I'm with the FBI," he explained, laying out the cover Center had provided. "I was sent here because the Bureau suspected Lester might be connected to older unsolved cases from other states. I've been monitoring the local investigation and we now know Lester's case is not related."

She moved her head from side to side in denial. "Are you saying you moved in next door to me on purpose? That you've been watching me?"

He hesitated a moment, hoping to lessen the impact of the single word, but it wasn't going to work. "Yes."

She drew her hand from his and turned away, but not before he saw the wetness shining in her eyes.

"But," he reached for her again, his fingers closing over her arm and pulling her gently back around to face him, "my job has nothing to do with this other connection between us."

She refused to look directly at him. "I don't know what you mean," she countered angrily. "What other connection?"

"This one." He drew her nearer and then he kissed her. It was what he wanted to do…what he needed to do.

She resisted at first but when his fingers threaded into her hair and pulled her closer still, she relented. Her mouth softened under his, her lips parted in invitation. He deepened the kiss, tasting her, wanting more, until every cell in his body detonated with need. She melted against him. Whimpered softly. He kissed her harder, allowing the rush of sensations to take control for just a few seconds.

He pulled back, his respiration uneven as if he'd run for miles. He licked his lips, loving the taste of her.

"I won't let anyone hurt you," he murmured. "Trust me."

And she did.

She didn't have to say the words. He read

her surrender in her eyes…felt it in the beat of her heart.

They were fully connected.

Again.

Chapter Seven

Château Garden Apartments
New Orleans

He stood in the darkest shadows of the court-yard. She was there...on the third floor. The French doors of her balcony overlooked this very courtyard.

Security was a joke. The police officers staking out her apartment were obviously asleep on the job. He'd gotten in with scarcely any effort and he'd been out of this part of the business for a very long time. But he had to see for himself...could trust no one else's judgment. Not even his closest adviser's.

He'd seen her. She was as beautiful as he had known she would be. He'd expected nothing less. If her gift proved to be as brilliant as her physical beauty, then she was truly magnificent. Discovering the depth of her abilities would require that he get closer…much closer.

But the Enforcer was in place already. He'd expected as much and yet it infuriated him. *She* was *his* creation. His masterpiece, just as the male no doubt was.

Center would send her other half—that he knew with certainty. The two had been designed to complement each other. Even now, he imagined that the bond drew them on every level. She would not fully comprehend what was happening, but the Enforcer would know.

Eve represented the only female created. She was immensely special. But O'Riley and Archer had deemed her a failure. A big mistake. He had been too careful, too meticulous, in his work. He had taken certain steps to ensure her perfection.

Fury whipped through him when he considered that Archer had ruined everything. The Enforcers were not created to suffer the same weaknesses as other humans. He had intended that they rise above those fragilities. But the Collective had overruled him, forced the change.

He had walked away, turned his back on all of it.

Years of bitterness had pushed him to retaliate—to fight for what was rightfully his. Despite all his efforts, his creations were still credited to others. His every attempt to regain what had been taken from him had failed.

He would not fail this time.

Nothing could stop him.

The male, Aidan, appeared on her balcony. He surveyed the courtyard, searching for the disruption he sensed in the fabric of the darkness. He listened for the slightest sound, his hearing so keen when he chose to listen closely that even a whispered sigh across the courtyard would be heard. He sniffed the air, every instinct warning of his enemy's presence.

Waylon Galen smiled. It was 2:00 a.m. She had allowed him to stay the night. Already the bond was reigniting, like fire in their souls. These two Enforcers were different from all the others. He had set aside risk analysis and pushed the envelope all the way, had overlooked nothing. Ensuring that their potential was far greater than any of the others, but only if they chose to hone their talents. The ability to turn down or off those dangerously elevated senses was absolutely essential.

Aidan and Eve were created to be together.

Their combined talents would be awesome. The male would show her the way. That needed to happen first. Too many years had passed for her to willingly accept her destiny. She would require prompting since her memory had likely been displaced. Galen knew how to make that happen regardless of whatever plans Center had. He would set a trap she could not run away from, one her protector could not ignore. To ensure his future success, he would need to show her how to tap into that special gift.

Galen wasn't foolish enough to believe he could control the two of them. The male would be entirely too powerful, too well-trained. But she would be easily contained, easily influenced. He knew answers to questions she hadn't even asked herself as of yet.

Answers that would change all that she believed to be right and true.

Aidan moved. Swung over the balcony railing and quickly climbed down the trellis. He faded into the darkness like a shadow, like a part of the night. Galen slipped back through the gate, hurried to his car and took off before the Enforcer could reach his position. He would not risk being caught now. He needed time to set things in motion, time to devise an infallible plan.

AIDAN WATCHED the gray sedan fly through the night. The headlights remained off until the driver had turned onto St. Charles. But he needed no license plate number or visual contact to identity his enemy.

Dr. Waylon Galen had made his first appearance.

Aidan performed a quick search of the grounds around the building. Though he was not particularly concerned that Galen had left anything behind, it was necessary to be certain. Galen would not want to harm the woman. His plans would require her to be alive. Aidan's fate would be another matter. But that did not concern him, either.

He sensed no other presence in the courtyard. A brief call to O'Riley was in order. Aidan withdrew his cellular phone from its clipped position at his waist and opened it. He entered O'Riley's number and waited for an answer. The man rarely slept. He was always on call.

"Galen is here. He knows her location."

O'Riley ordered him to carry on with Operation Prophecy as previously outlined.

Aidan put his phone away and checked the small handgun strapped to his ankle. Enforcers not primarily used as assassins only carried weapons when absolute necessity required it. Their powers of stealth and unparalleled strength allowed for disabling their targets with other methods.

O'Riley had deemed an external weapon necessary for this operation.

A rush of energy slammed into Aidan, then receded, dragging his mind back to…her. His gaze went immediately to the balcony, to the open French doors. She was dreaming… reaching out to him with her mind.

He scaled the trellis in seconds, hopped over the balcony railing and moved through the wide-open doors. He crossed the living room, stood in the open doorway of her bedroom. Closing his eyes he braced himself against the wood frame and opened his mind to her…allowing her access. He could not see her dreams unless she showed him, but he could feel her distress, her desperation. She needed him and she didn't know how to connect on that level yet, didn't know how to touch him the way he could touch her. She'd let him in all the way that once. He had no choice but to wait for her invitation now.

Let me in, Darby, he whispered silently. *Let me in.*

SHE TRIED TO WAKE UP from the dream. Darby kept telling herself not to look, to open her eyes and wake up. But she couldn't. She couldn't find her way back.

He was there…somewhere. She could hear him calling to her. But they weren't alone.

She felt the evil. Felt it trying to seep into her pores. She had to fight…to run. She ran harder… faster, but it was like everything had lapsed into slow motion. The faster she ran, the slower she moved through the dream.

He was going to catch her.

There were trees all around her…a forest. The route she followed was dark and foreboding.

Voices. She heard voices. Crying. The children were crying for her. They wanted to go home. She could take them home. All she had to do was find them.

A face zoomed into focus right in front of her. She stumbled…fell onto her hands and knees. She screamed at him to leave her alone but it was Jerry Lester and he wouldn't listen.

One, two, I'm coming for you. Three, four better lock your door. I'm coming for you, Darby Shepard. You can't hide from me. We have a score to settle. These children belong to me!

She scrambled to her feet once more and started to run…had to run. He would catch her if she didn't run. His face faded, but another image took its place. The men in white coats. They poked and prodded, tested her, made her keep trying…but she couldn't. She couldn't do what they wanted or she would never get away. They would keep her forever.

She never wanted to go back there.

Never. Never.

She had to find the children. They wanted to go home. She could find them…she'd found the others. Not now…another time. She wasn't strong enough now. Run…she had to keep running.

She saw him from a long way off. Standing in the mist, moving toward her. He was tall and dark, the white mist swirled around his long legs. He came closer and closer and she couldn't move.

Aidan.

Her dream man.

He had said he could protect her. He would keep her safe. She could trust him. He'd

kissed her and she'd felt something strong…
something familiar.

In her dream, he stopped a few feet away
and held out his hand.

She moved toward him. It was only a few
feet. But the faster she ran the farther away he
looked. She called his name. Reached for him.
But he only moved farther away without actually moving at all. He was so far away now
she could scarcely see him. Her heart hammered in her chest. She felt too tired to keep
running; yet if she lost sight of him, she knew
she would not survive the coming battle. She
needed him. But he was just out of reach.

"Aidan!"

Darby bolted upright and fought to catch
her breath. Her side ached as if she'd run a
marathon. Perspiration dampened her skin.

Aidan was at her side before her eyes could
adjust to the dark. "It was only a dream," he
murmured.

She hugged her arms around her knees and
rocked herself gently. "I need to see where
the children are," she whispered, her mind
still reeling from the images in the dream.
"They want to go home."

The tears would not be denied. It didn't
matter how hard she tried. She couldn't stop

it, just like she couldn't stop the things that were about to happen. He had escaped. He knew her name, what she looked like. With every fiber of her being, she knew he would not just run; he would want his vengeance first.

Better lock your door.

But Aidan was here.

He would protect her.

Strong arms went around her and she felt safe.

The FBI had sent him here. Though she knew that there was more involved here than his job…an attraction…a bond. He wanted to keep her safe. She knew that as surely as she knew Lester would come for her. He would find her…reach her somehow.

"Would you like me to get you a glass of wine? Something to help you sleep?"

Aidan's gentle voice, so deep and alluring, made her want to sink into his arms, to be one with him completely. He felt so familiar… like a part of her. She pushed the unrealistic concepts away. Stress, she told herself. It was playing havoc with her ability to reason.

She needed someone and all her friends had deserted her. He was here, willing and ready to hold her, protect her. That had to be

the connection she felt. She *needed* him…
that was all it could be.

"Wine would be good, I think."

He drew back, smiled down at her.

Her heart thumped against her sternum.
He was so beautiful.

Her eyes had adjusted to the dark now.
Still, it seemed odd that she could see the details of his handsome face so well. A hint of
moonlight filtered through the sheer drapes,
but not much.

He pushed up from the bed and left the
room. She sat very still for a time, completely
disarmed by the way he moved. She closed
her eyes and remembered the way he'd
kissed her. Had shown her the depth of the
connection between them. Not for a second
had she been able to deny how he'd touched
her. It felt right…safe…like home.

"Get a grip, Darby," she muttered. Getting
any more deeply involved with a stranger, no
matter how right it felt, was not a smart move.

She'd already asked him to spend the
night…on the couch, of course. She didn't
usually behave so irrationally. Not once in her
entire life had a man spent the night in her
apartment. She tried to remember when was
the last time she'd had sex. Too long ago to

recall. At his place and she'd left immediately afterward, regretting the act even before she had her clothes back on. The two times she'd allowed herself to become physically intimate with a man had felt wholly wrong. She told herself it was all those Sunday mornings in church with her parents, but she was beginning to think now that maybe she just hadn't met the right man.

She had a feeling she would not regret anything that happened between her and Aidan. But, erring on the side of caution was always the smartest route to take. She'd learned that long ago as well. Had made it a steadfast rule.

Though she didn't always manage to stick by her golden rule.

She threw back the covers and went in search of her robe. She had one that matched this gown, the only sexy one she owned, somewhere. Throwing on the terry cloth one would ruin the look entirely.

A single lamp lit the living room as she went in search of her brave protector. A chill shivered over her and she tightened the sash to her white silk robe.

Aidan emerged from the kitchen, two glasses of wine in his hands. He offered her the one in his right, then sipped the other.

"Thank you."

She took her wine and settled on the couch. He settled in a chair directly across from her, his dark form nearly disappearing into the deep navy of the upholstery.

"Do you want to talk about it?"

She considered saying no for a while but then decided it couldn't hurt.

"Lester was after me. The children were calling for me." She shrugged, then took a long swallow of her wine. "Then you showed up, but I couldn't reach you."

"That wasn't on purpose, I can assure you," he said with a smile.

She smiled back, then stared at the pale liquid in her glass. She'd once read a book about the meaning of dreams. Too bad she couldn't recall any of it now.

"Anything else?"

She met his gaze once more. Those dark, dark eyes sparkled with challenge. He wanted to hear more, dared her to share the whole truth with him.

Somehow she couldn't resist.

"There were other men." She thought about the men in the white coats. "Doctors, maybe. They wanted something, but I'm not sure what they signify."

"You've dreamed of them before."

She nodded, wondering how he could know. Or maybe he'd just made a good guess.

"Are you afraid of these men?"

His tone never changed, placating, soothing. He made talking to him so easy.

"Terrified," she admitted. "I think they have something to do with my past."

"Your past?"

There was an utter stillness about him, yet there was also an energy emanating that made her feel warm, secure.

"I was adopted when I was ten. I can't remember much before that. But those men in the white lab coats are a part of it somehow."

"Have you tried regression therapy? Hypnosis of any sort?"

She shrugged. "I've thought about it. Even read up on self-hypnosis. But I just never followed through."

"You don't remember anything else that might be relevant?"

"A place. I think it was called Center, but I'm not sure."

"Have you researched what it could mean?"

Suddenly she felt uneasy. There was something different in his tone now, a subtle edge that disturbed her.

"You think I should?" she asked, certain that she must be mistaken. Lack of sleep was obviously taking its toll.

"Not really. It could mean nothing at all."

"Or it could be some place where I stayed before being adopted," she countered, surprised by his change in attitude on the subject.

He leaned forward and braced his forearms on his widespread knees. He looked straight into her eyes, his own surprisingly unyielding. "Some things we're better off not knowing."

For the first time since she'd met Special Agent Aidan Tanner, she felt uncomfortable in his presence.

"Some things are too painful," he added gently, his gaze softening as well.

Setting her glass aside, she planted her elbow on the arm of the sofa and rested her chin in her hand. "You're right. It could be very painful. Instinct tells me that it all means something. I just don't know what." She ran a hand through her hair. "I learned to trust my instincts a long time ago."

He deposited his glass onto the table and stood. Her gaze followed his movements as he came to sit on the sofa with her. Anticipation shivered through her.

"And what do your instincts tell you about

me?" He draped one arm on the back of the sofa behind her and waited for her answer, that piercing gaze never leaving her face for an instant.

"Do you always get this close to your suspects, Agent Tanner?" she asked frankly.

"This is the first time." He tucked a strand of hair behind her ear. "And, for the record, you're not a suspect."

She had to smile. "Are you sure you haven't let things get personal before? You seem awfully good at this to be a...*virgin,*" she suggested. Whatever possessed her at that moment to be so bold she would never know, but she couldn't slow the momentum. This was headed way out of control and she just didn't possess the willpower to stop it.

He lowered his head, bringing his lips so close to hers that she could feel their sensual pull. "You're the only woman I've ever wanted to break the rules for," he whispered. "I don't think I'm going to be able to stop this without your assistance."

Her throat constricted with yearning. Her whole body heated, longed to feel his lips against hers. "I'm afraid you're out of luck, then, because I'm completely vulnerable where you're concerned."

He kissed her slowly, tenderly. She wanted more. He drew back at the same instant that she decided to throw caution to the wind.

"We both need sleep," he murmured against her lips. "We'll finish this another time."

He rose and strode to the French doors. He opened the doors wide and went out onto the balcony. The breeze moved around him, played with his hair, reached all the way into the room to whisper across her skin.

Maybe he was right. Sleep was what they both needed. And just maybe she'd get lucky and dream about him. This time she would find a way to reach him.

Center Ghost Mountain

GOVERNOR REMINGTON did not look pleased.

He didn't like the way this was going.

"What if that psycho gets to her first?" He paced the length of O'Riley's office once more. "What then?"

"He won't." O'Riley knew the psycho he referred to was Lester, the serial killer who'd escaped lockup less than twenty-four hours ago.

"How can you be so sure?" Remington threw his hands up, then planted them firmly at his waist. "Can we take that chance?"

"We have to." O'Riley settled one hip on the corner of his desk. "Aidan will protect her."

"But this is his first solo operation," Remington argued. "He's different from the others. He uses the power of his mind more than his physical strength."

"That's right," O'Riley agreed. "But that's an advantage, not a disadvantage."

The governor paused and glared at O'Riley. "If she remembers everything, this whole operation could blow up. She might become unstable."

"Aidan knows how to handle the situation. He's prepared for every scenario."

"Meanwhile we just wait it out," Remington countered. "We don't send in anyone else. We don't do anything. Galen is there. We have to stop him. To hell with Lester. It's Galen we really have to worry about."

O'Riley clasped his hands in front of him and strove for patience. "That's true. But it's also the most important reason to leave things just as they are."

Remington finally collapsed into a chair. "What the hell does that mean?"

"There's too big a risk that Darby Shepard would sense the presence of a second Enforcer. We can't take that chance. Aidan can provide sufficient protection."

"But what about Galen?" he demanded. "Who's going to stop him? Aidan can't play protector and aggressor at the same time."

O'Riley smiled. Some guys just didn't see the forest for the trees. He'd just have to spell it out for him. "Our ultimate goal is to get Galen while protecting Center."

Remington made a dramatic "go on" gesture.

"He's a slippery bastard. We might not ever be able to catch him in the usual manner. He knows too much…knows the Enforcers. But we have him at a disadvantage right now."

"How's that?" Remington asked, his curiosity piqued now.

"He wants our girl. She's the only vulnerable link to Center. He'll come after her, no question. If we wait, lure him in on our terms, we'll get him."

"Use her as bait," Remington stated for clarification.

"That's right. What better way to catch a man who thinks he's God than with his own creation?"

"Can Aidan do this alone?"

"I believe so."

"And if we lose them both as a result of this strategy?"

"As long as we get Galen and Center is protected, we've accomplished our mission."

"So both he and the girl are expendable?"

O'Riley shrugged. "Aren't we all?"

"You're expecting that special bond that once existed between the two of them to carry them through this ordeal, aren't you?"

"I'm not only expecting it, I'm counting on it."

If Remington only knew how true that was. The woman was the key to far more than he knew.

That was one secret O'Riley intended to keep.

Chapter Eight

New Orleans
Sunday afternoon

Traffic was light on I-10 as they made their way to the West Bank exit across the Crescent City Connection Bridge. From there, General de Gaulle East led across the Intercoastal Waterway Bridge. A right on Louisiana Highway 406 and less than thirty minutes after leaving her apartment, they had reached English Village, the community where her parents' home stood empty.

Aidan drove his sporty black sedan. Two doors, low to the ground, sleek and sexy with tinted windows and four on the floor. Hot and fast.

So, she mused, he was one of those guys who liked to shift gears, pushing an engine for all it was worth before rocketing to the next level. She should have known there would be a racy side to this quiet, enigmatic man.

Contrastingly, the only vehicle she owned was the old Cadillac she had inherited from her parents. It stayed in the garage at their home, gathering dust more often than not. A car was just in the way in a busy city like New Orleans.

Aidan stopped at the security gate to the residential community long enough for Darby to show her ID. A gated neighborhood located on the riverbank, with numerous parks and family-oriented amenities, the Village had been a great place to grow up. Safe, prestigious. But it was the nights she'd spent in the city with her friends that she recalled most about her childhood. The secret strolls along the cobblestoned streets of the French Quarter and adrenaline-pumping adventures in the cemeteries. Her parents would absolutely have suffered heart failure if they'd had any idea.

The vibrancy of the city had been like lifeblood to Darby. Even now when she ventured too far away from New Orleans proper, she felt lost and out of sorts.

"Take a right there." She pointed to an upcoming cross street.

Aidan slowed and took the turn.

"The second house on the left."

He pulled into the driveway and Darby immediately experienced an ache in the center of her chest. Even after five years, it hurt to come here.

The Georgian-style home offered every amenity. More than four thousand square feet of elegance. Her friends couldn't understand why she refused to live here. But she would some day…maybe. If she could beat down her addiction to the steamy, gritty world of New Orleans.

Aidan had opened her door before she'd realized he'd gotten out of the vehicle. Just another of her bad habits. Daydreaming…always lost in thought.

The gardener had already put in the fall flowers. As she moved closer to the house, the sight of those colorful blooms made her think of Jerry Lester and his sickness. Revulsion shuddered through her. Coming here was probably a good thing with him on the loose. She didn't like wondering if he would discover her new address or if he would risk taking another child.

Darby glanced over her shoulder as the police cruiser parked at the curb in front of her house. They had insisted on staying close by, which added another layer of protection. The officer in charge hadn't asked about her friend and she hadn't offered any information. Aidan had said that he'd been involved on some level with the ongoing case. Detective Willis was likely well aware of Aidan's presence in her life. Still, she'd be sure to mention it later.

She was very lucky to have a man like him on her side.

She unlocked the front door and disarmed the home's security system. The vaguely unpleasant smell of disuse assailed her nostrils. Though she kept the house cool in the summer and warm in the winter, there was still a lingering staleness. The lack of steam rising from showers…the varied and distinct aromas that accompanied the preparation of family meals…perfumes and body sprays. All of those things were missing, leaving the house to smell like an unused closet rather than a home where life happened. Those same old sentimental feelings tugged at her emotions. When would she stop missing them so?

Aidan closed and locked the door. "Very nice," he commented as he surveyed the soaring entry hall.

She considered the massive curving staircase and the towering second-story landing and wondered if his childhood home or homes had been similar to this. Her parents had not been exactly wealthy, comfortable more than anything. They were older when they'd elected to adopt, their finances in good order with wise investments. When they'd died, there hadn't been that much money to inherit, but there was the property, which was more than enough. She would trade it in a heartbeat to have them back in her life.

Darby tossed her purse onto the bench part of the antique coat rack stationed a few feet from the door. "Well, let's get to it."

She and Aidan had discussed how best for her to look into her past. He had offered to go through his own sources but she had declined, feeling more comfortable without the involvement of others. What she didn't tell him was her fear of putting her name out there where the wrong people might see it or somehow have access. She'd never really bothered to dig through the family files, not in depth anyway. All the estate documents had been filed appropriately, not requiring her to do any real searching. Since the accident she'd had no reason to think about her past…not really.

Not until now, anyway.

She would start with her father's study.

The richly paneled, masculinely decorated room drew a smile to her lips. Her father had worked at home most of the time, choosing to be with his family as much as possible. His position as board member for one of Louisiana's premier development companies had allowed him that luxury.

She settled into his big leather chair and started with the files in his desk, then moved to the credenza and eventually on to the file cabinets that lined one wall. Drawer after drawer, folder after folder. She found nothing related to her adoption.

The file detailing her trips to the doctor and dentist. All routine checkups, never an illness or even a cavity. Eye exams—20/20 vision. Nothing out of the ordinary.

She looked up and found Aidan enthralled with family photo albums. Her mother had meticulously kept the matching albums up to date, each labeled with the years they contained. Darby was five years behind...pictures tucked in drawers or wherever they happened to land after she picked them up from the One-Hour Photo.

Her gaze dropped back to the medical file

in her hand. "Do you realize I've never been sick a day in my life? Not once. And only one broken bone...not the first stitch."

He looked at her over the top of the album currently holding his attention. "That would please most people."

She tucked the folder back into place and closed the final drawer, disgusted with her search. "I'm not complaining, it just seems odd."

He shrugged. "Not so odd. I've never been sick. Perfect health is a good thing."

"But unusual." She folded one arm over her middle and braced the other one there so that she could tap her chin. Maybe she'd call her father's attorney. She hadn't talked to him in years. Maybe now he would tell her what he knew about how her parents had come to adopt her.

"Come here."

Aidan's voice elicited a pang of longing, made her want to listen to him speak for hours. Her gaze moved to the dark one focused on her. "What?"

He beckoned to her with the long fingers of one hand. "Come."

She pushed to her feet, skirted the desk and sidled up next to him, unable to resist taking in his tall frame from head to toe and back. His penchant for black fit so well with her love of the mystical, her relentless obsession with the city she loved so much. She wanted to know more about him…to know everything.

"Tell me about this." He pointed to a picture of her dressed in her senior prom gown. "What was the special occasion?"

Aidan listened as she told him about her senior prom and how she'd gone with a guy who was just a friend, hadn't managed to snag herself a boyfriend. He watched her animated expressions as she spoke. Followed the movement of her lips, his own hungry for the taste of her. He wondered what it would be like to dance…to hold her in his arms as the other man had done at her prom.

They grabbed armfuls of the albums and retreated to the family room, where she curled up on a sectional sofa next to him and led him through her life with the Shepards in pictures. She'd gone from a sullen unhappy child at ten to a breathtakingly beautiful girl at twelve.

Aidan considered his own life during those same stages as she moved through her well-documented past. She'd had many friends, had participated in numerous extracurricular activities. Dance lessons, piano lessons. She had blossomed into a young woman so fascinating he could scarcely take his eyes off her. Not once in the life she recalled had she taken a self-defense class or weapons training. Her life had been nothing at all like his.

How could she have grown up in such a different world, the bond between them severed by geography and culture, and still draw him this way? He knew with certainty that Center had miscalculated the strength of the connection. He recognized that he was too close, but he refused to allow the possibility of another Enforcer being sent to replace him. His objectivity might not be fully intact but he would not lose sight of the mission.

"Oh, my gosh, it's getting late."

Aidan followed her gaze to the wall of windows that faced west. The sun had dropped low in the sky. Five or five-thirty already. It would be dark soon. In an hour, perhaps.

"I'll help you put the albums away." They both reached for the one they'd just looked at. Their hands touched and warmth spread through him. Now was not the time to pick up where they'd left off so early this morning, but he was very tempted.

She looked away from his steady gaze and hurriedly gathered an armful of the albums. He picked up the rest and followed her back to her father's study.

When the last album had been replaced, she said, "I need to get something from my old room. I'll be right back."

She didn't wait for a response but she got one anyway. "I'll come with you."

She glanced over her shoulder without slowing. "As long as you don't give me any grief over the color scheme."

He climbed the staircase a few steps behind her, enjoying the view more than he should. He felt certain she would not be amused if she were to see his thoughts at the moment. Every muscle in his body had gone rigid with desire. Willpower had never been an issue for him. He could go for days without sleep or nourishment. But he was not at all sure how long he would last without sharing complete physical intimacy with her.

Turning to walk backward along the upstairs hall, she warned as she neared what must be the door to her room, "Don't say a word." Then she swung back toward her destination, her long hair swirling around her, and disappeared through the open door.

He laughed when he stood in the middle of her room. White wicker furniture and tie-dyed curtains and linens. Posters of rock stars or maybe movie stars lined the walls. It was definitely different from what he'd expected.

"I warned you," she said from inside the closet.

"You warned me not to say a word. You didn't say I couldn't laugh," he corrected as he went to the bureau and studied the framed photographs of her with some of the same friends he'd seen in photographs downstairs. She smiled a lot. He liked her smile.

"I'm ready." She tugged her hair loose from the button-up sweater she'd pulled on. "I'd almost forgotten this old sweater until I saw it in some of the pictures." She hugged the sides around her. "It's my lucky sweater."

Her lucky sweater lacked any real appeal. Bland gray and rather shapeless, the material looked to be wool or something like it. A couple of buttons were missing. He had to admit he'd never seen a lucky sweater; maybe they all looked like that.

"Let's go," she said, clearly pleased with her rediscovered treasure. "I have calls to make."

She took his hand and led him from the room.

"I'm going to call my dad's attorney and

see if he remembers anything about the adoption." She looked up at him as they descended the stairs. "Surely he wouldn't have a problem sharing whatever he knows with me now."

Aidan pushed the corners of his mouth into a facsimile of a smile. "Good idea."

He didn't see the point in bursting her bubble. Her father's attorney would know nothing. According to her file at Center, her adoption had been handled personally by Director O'Riley through one of Center's attorneys. It would take two lifetimes to wade through the red tape the attorney had wrapped around the case. That transaction would never be traced back to Center.

Darby waved at the policemen as she settled into the passenger seat of the car Center had arranged for him to use. The officers looked ready for a shift change. According to Aidan's calculations, that would likely occur as soon as they arrived back at her apartment.

Darby relaxed into the leather seat and hugged her sweater more tightly around her. She stole a peek at her chauffeur and smiled. He was so cool. Nothing seemed to faze him, not even this ungodly sweater. He just went with the flow. Whatever she wanted was fine by him. She decided it had to be part of his job. No real guy would have fun flipping through old family photos all afternoon on a beautiful day like today. She suddenly wondered if he golfed or played racquetball. No. He didn't look like the type. If he participated in any sports, it would be something brutal like hockey or soccer.

She really liked that polished yet tough exterior.

As they neared the Intercoastal Waterway Bridge, pain abruptly seared through her brain. She sucked in a sharp breath and squeezed her eyes shut against the intensity of it.

"What's wrong?"

Dark. Water. She could smell the swamp.

"Darby."

Trees dripping with moss.

She gripped the armrests and panted to fight the building pain.

Voices. Too indistinct to comprehend.

Then it was gone.

The episode left her fighting for breath, her heart pumping fiercely.

"Tell me what just happened."

She held up a hand in hopes he would give

her a minute to work past her body's automatic responses to the fierce pain.

Another slash of light momentarily blinded her.

Voices.

Clearer this time…louder.

The children.

Crying out to her.

She blinked to focus and dragged in another gulp of air. "Aidan…I…"

Come back.

Come back, please come back.

"We have to go back…"

"Back where?" He glanced from the road to her.

Only when he spoke did she realize she'd said the words out loud.

"There's…something I need to do."

The police cruiser followed close behind them. What would they think about her sudden need to follow the voices in her head? They would call it in and some reporter monitoring the police band would hear her name and rush to get the latest scoop. She couldn't go through that again. How could she risk telling the cops what she felt?

Darby wasn't sure she wanted to know the answer to that one. This was something she needed to do alone. She cast a long, assessing gaze at the man behind the wheel. Well, maybe not completely alone. The FBI had sent him to keep an eye on the case and ultimately her.

"When we get into the city, is there some way we can give the cops the slip? Maybe pretend we've—"

"Why would we want to give the *slip* to your bodyguards?"

She couldn't quite read his tone, something between noncommittal and suspicious.

How did she explain this without sounding like a fool? Whatever she felt at the moment was different from her dreams. She was wide awake, for one thing, and she felt an extreme urgency rather than the usual dread or panic. She had to do this.

"There's something I have to do."

His gaze met hers for a moment. "Related to Lester's case?"

She nodded.

For three seconds that turned into ten, she was certain he intended to deny her request.

"All right. This is what we'll do."

THEY HAD WAITED until it was dark.

When they'd returned to the city, Aidan

had made a show of dropping her off at her borrowed apartment and then driving away. He'd parked his car three blocks beyond the opposite side of the apartment building from where the cops had set up their stakeout. He'd given her one instruction before leaving: dress in dark clothing.

She'd dug through her friend's closet until she found black jeans and a navy sweatshirt. Black hiking boots had completed her getup. Her friend wouldn't mind…she hoped. If Darby ruined anything, she'd just have to replace it. She'd only brought a few changes of clothes with her to her friend's home. She hadn't expected to stay this long.

When night came, she'd slipped out of the apartment, leaving the living room light and the television on, and took the stairs down to the lobby. She'd packed a flashlight and a few other necessities into a small backpack, which she draped over one shoulder. A frown creased her brow when she didn't find Aidan.

She moved quietly toward the communal laundry room. He'd said they would go out the side door and slip away via the alley between this house and the next. Sounded good to her. She just wasn't sure where her partner in crime was at the moment. She couldn't help wondering if he'd changed his mind. Or if something had happened.

Her heart jolted at the idea of his being hurt in any way. If Lester had learned her new address…if he was watching…

"I've been waiting."

Darby barely clamped her hand over her mouth to trap the squeal that lodged in her throat.

Aidan stepped from the dark shadows in the far corner of the room. "Sorry," he offered. "I thought you knew I was here."

Now how would she have known? Instead of asking, she tamped down her annoyance and headed toward the side door.

"Guess not," he murmured as he cut in front of her to be the first out the door.

That would have annoyed her as well if she hadn't known the move had been made to protect her.

In the dark alley, he took her hand and walked quickly toward the end that opened into the street where he'd parked his car. Once he had ensured the coast was clear, they covered the three blocks in no time. Darby felt the power of his muscular body as he pushed quickly forward with hardly any effort. She, on the other hand, had worked hard to keep up with him.

In the car, he asked, "Where are we going?"

She thought about that for a moment. Remembered the last time she'd been there when she'd led the police to his hideout. "Back to the water—to the swamp. He likes it there."

He pushed the gearshift into position and rolled away from the curb. "Is this the same place where the police found him before?"

She nodded. "That's where we need to go…only deeper into the bayou. I know they're there. Hidden away so no one can find them." A new kind of fear eddied through her as another frightening possibility zoomed to the forefront of her thoughts. "I hadn't even considered that he might be hanging around there somewhere."

"He won't risk getting too close."

Aidan made the statement with such certainty. She wondered how he could be so sure.

Before she could question his conclusion, he said, "The police will have crawled all over the place. Probably still have a team watching the same way they're watching you."

She hadn't thought of that either.

Seems she hadn't thought of much.

Hurry.

The urgency nudged her again. It didn't matter what the police or Lester did or didn't do. She had to do this. There wasn't a choice.

Forty-five long, gut-wrenching minutes passed with the anticipation and urgency mounting in Darby before they reached the small town where they would be required to leave land behind. The water forked around the small fishing village, leading deep into the swamps...to where they needed to go.

"Park there." She directed him to a small lot where tourists converged to venture out into the swamp. "They keep the boats in the back." Real Cajun Guides, a sign boasted. She got out of the car, not waiting for Aidan to come around and open her door.

He looked at her across the top of the car, the sliver of moon providing barely enough light to make out his features in the gloomy darkness.

"So we're going to steal one," he suggested. She didn't miss the note of amusement hiding just beneath the surface of his skepticism.

"No, Agent Tanner," she said sweetly, "we're going to borrow one."

Aidan did smile then, couldn't hold it back

any longer. She definitely had the determination one would expect in an Enforcer. She had the talents he'd expected as well. Disuse and lack of training had rendered them unreliable. But they were there just the same.

He walked cautiously toward the looming metal building, its siding rusty with age. A place of business would surely have some sort of security system.

When he rounded the corner, he crossed paths with the security on duty.

A low growl emanated from the big dog, its breed not readily identifiable but its intent crystal clear.

"Steady, boy," he said softly. Security patrolled with similar animals at Center, but Aidan rarely encountered one without its handler. Yet he felt no fear. He knew techniques to disable the animal without doing permanent damage if the need arose. "Have you made this animal's acquaintance before?" he asked of his companion, careful to keep his voice low and nonthreatening.

"Here you go, fella," Darby murmured to the dog.

Sniffing, the dog cocked his head to one side and moved closer to her. She held out what appeared to be a large bone of suspect origin. The dog latched on to it and loped away to ensure privacy while he devoured it. Well, that answered his question plainly enough. Obviously she had encountered the animal previously which was why she'd known to bring a treat.

"He was here before," she said when her gaze collided with his. "He gave the police a hard time until his owner took him inside."

Aidan nodded. He could definitely imagine that very scenario.

"This way."

Against his better judgment, he allowed her to lead. Her stealth surprised him. He wondered just how good she would be had she been subjected to the same training as him. Quite good, he estimated.

She surveyed the offerings a moment before pointing to what looked to be a ten-foot pirogue. The long, slender vessel was similar to a canoe but more efficiently designed. The pirogue rocked as they climbed aboard. She tossed her backpack on a pile of crawfish nets. He removed the loop of rope that anchored it to the dock at the same time that she reached for the push-pole.

With a succinct shake of his head, he took it from her. She surrendered without argument and pointed south. He pushed away from the dock, the sinuous feel of the boat sliding soundlessly through the black water.

The voices had drawn her here. Though he couldn't hear them, he sensed her urgency. Felt her desperate need to find the remains of Lester's victims.

Like Aidan, she had a mission. To see that those children made it home.

Unfamiliar emotions welled inside him as he considered how much she was willing to risk.

Her willingness to sacrifice was what had brought her here…would cost her more than she imagined if he learned she was hiding the truth.

He surveyed the dark primordial world that lay before them. Lester wanted to hurt her. Aidan could feel his hatred, his desire for vengeance in the heavy air. He'd passed this way…not long ago.

But Jerry Lester was inconsequential in the scheme of things.

He was already dead. He just didn't know it yet.

Chapter Nine

Darby could only hope that the big old ham bone she'd found frozen in the freezer held no sentimental value for her friend. Knowing her friend's penchant for fifteen-bean soup, Darby assumed she'd been saving it for making soup. But she couldn't be sure. In any event, she had been gone for six months, had six to go. Who wanted a ham bone that old in their soup?

Lacking any real culinary talent, Darby could only pray that ham bones didn't age the same way wine did. Thankfully, her distraction had worked; the watchdog had taken the bait.

She scanned the bank on either side of the dark, inky water. Not that she could see much. The moon was scarcely a sliver in the black velvet canvas of the sky. But she'd been here before, knew that rickety shacks on stilts dotted the shore here and there. Rusty metal boathouses rose up from the water like swamp monsters. Shrimp boats and other smaller vessels sat as still as stone upon the glassy surface. The folks who lived here represented a different breed. Some were good, hardworking types who never bothered anyone and who had simply chosen a simpler way of life. Others were barely a cut above criminals, poachers and the like, thriving in the world where alligators ruled.

The waterway branched off again and again. Each time she gestured vaguely, Aidan somehow seemed to know what she meant, even in the consuming darkness.

A gauzy white mist drifted like smoke on the water's surface, winding through the gnarled, moss-laden cypress trees. The chirps and trill of insects and the song of frogs filtered through the night. The air was heavy with scents, some sweet, some definitely not.

The swamp was in reality a place of natural beauty. During the day or on a night blessed by a full moon, one would see great blue herons and tall, slender egrets as they fished along the bank. One might also see other wild animals such as snakes, turtles, raccoons, black bears, red wolves, deer and exotic birds.

And then there were the ever-present alligators. More than 500,000, according to the latest statistics. The thought had no more flickered through her mind than right next to the pirogue she sensed the distinct ripple through the water of one of the primitive creatures. She shuddered.

A whoosh of energy went through her and she knew they were getting close.

Close to that simple rectangular cabin where Lester had held the children. The bastard had taunted them, had allowed them to go without food and water until they'd pleaded with him, done anything he'd asked for a mere sip of water.

Thank God he hadn't sexually abused any of them. Lester's problem wasn't about sex; it was about power. The children belonged to him, were his possessions. With his twisted personality and bizarre perception of life, the chance of having any of his own was, thankfully, nil. He'd become obsessed with other people's children, had probably thought he could make them his own weird kind of family. His need to rule had gotten out of control with little Christina Fairgate and she'd ended up dead. Like the others...out there somewhere calling to Darby.

But she knew what the shrinks who'd evaluated him the few days he'd stayed in jail hadn't uncovered just yet. Lester's problem went way back—he was trying hard to make a family be what he thought it should be. The extreme measures he'd been willing to go to in order to accomplish that end spoke volumes about his past. Maybe he'd been abused in some way as a child.

She shoved aside the theories. Regardless of what had or hadn't happened in his past, he was a damned psycho who didn't deserve to live. He'd been playing at this serial killer thing for years without getting caught. It wasn't until he'd gone into the "escalating" phase that he'd screwed up. All that time, he'd done his hunting far away from his home territory. Impatience had spawned sloppiness and he'd started seeking his prey right in his own backyard. And Darby had picked up on his presence. When he took a child close to her, it had been the final push her heightened senses had needed.

The pirogue rounded a turn in the waterway and the rickety old cabin came into view. Positioned a couple feet off the ground to protect against flooding, it looked ready to collapse. A stovepipe stuck up from the roof, jaunted at an odd angle. Pots and pots of blooming flowers overflowed on every available surface.

Dread pooled in Darby's stomach. She felt sick, repulsed by the place. Though she knew it was just a house, that the evil had come from the man, not the place. Still, seeing his lair again made her want to heave. The police should have burned it to the ground...but it was evidence. Yellow crime scene tape was draped haphazardly around the perimeter of the structure.

But it hadn't stopped him from crossing that line.

He'd been here.

She knew—felt it all the way to her bones.

She closed her eyes and listened for the voices that would lead her.

The instant the pirogue bumped into the lopsided dock, she stood. The boat bobbed, making her stomach dip.

"Wait."

Aidan set the push-pole aside and tied off the boat.

Darby didn't want to wait. She wanted to find them. Good sense screamed at her to wait until daylight. But she didn't need the light...she had the voices. They would lead her. The urge felt stronger than ever before. So powerful. So consuming. She couldn't not do this.

How could she have possessed this kind of…gift…all this time and not known the full extent of it?

Because you hadn't wanted to see. You refused to look.

The pull was more than she could bear. She couldn't wait.

Bracing her foot against the decaying wood, she pulled herself up onto the dock. Aidan reached for her, keeping her steady when she would have swayed.

He held her back when she started for the house. He didn't speak but he was scanning the area, as if he suspected someone or something was out there.

Where were the police, she suddenly wondered? Aidan was right. They should be here.

He was here.

The realization hit her with enough force to rock her. Aidan's strong arm steadied her.

"He's here," she murmured, her heart stalling in her chest.

"I know."

She opened her mouth to ask how he could

know but he started moving forward, propelling her alongside him.

The night sounds amplified, pressing in around her. Her imagination she told herself—not real.

She thought about Bigfoot and all the old pirate stories she'd heard. Even the ones about some parts of the bayou being cursed by a voodoo queen. Foolish. Just stories passed down from generation to generation. Stories where fact and legend collided.

Then she thought about the gossip that bodies of previous residents were buried in unmarked graves throughout the swamp. She imagined there was some truth to that one.

But the children…they didn't belong here. She had to make sure they were found.

At the rear corner of the cabin, Aidan detained her once more, bent down and pulled a small handgun from an ankle holster. She blinked, stunned that she hadn't considered before that an FBI agent would carry a gun. He seemed so capable without one.

Moving on autopilot now, she didn't resist when he ushered her behind him before rounding the corner.

At first, she didn't see the body sprawled

in the thick grasses. But something, a raccoon maybe, scurried away from where the man lay.

Darby's heart rushed into her throat, sticking there like a tennis ball.

Aidan crouched down, his attention divided between their surroundings and the body on the ground. He checked for a pulse and shook his head. She exhaled a shaky breath, forcing her heart back into her chest where it started to pound frantically.

He reached into the man's pocket and pulled out an ID. Cop. Detective. NOPD.

Aidan's head came up. His posture stiffened ever so slightly, but Darby noticed. She felt it, too—the subtle shift in the atmosphere. The sudden silence of the nocturnal creatures. Dead silence.

He came here for something.

The rush of the epiphany shook her.

Aidan's gaze collided with hers, as if he understood what she'd just experienced.

Impossible.

"He's waiting for something," she whispered.

"There would be more than one officer on duty at a stakeout like this," Aidan commented, his full attention focused on the encroaching trees and the eerie stillness.

While she still turned over this newest information, Aidan was suddenly next to her, tugging her toward that ominous tree line. She wanted to ask him what he thought he was doing. But she knew from his brutal grasp and relentless pace that there was no time for questions. Whatever he'd seen or heard, she hadn't sensed it. Hadn't experienced any warning of danger.

Her so-called extra sense was unreliable. Dammit.

A welcome surge of reckless anger solidified her determination.

She would make it work. She'd done it before with Madam Talia's help. She'd gotten this far on her own tonight.

The need to close her eyes and focus was very nearly overwhelming, but how could she do that with Aidan dragging her through the woods?

Her boot snagged on a root. She pitched forward but Aidan caught her. Righted her and kept pushing forward.

She wanted to ask him where the hell they were going, but she didn't dare speak.

Safety.

The word slammed into her brain like a speeding bullet.

Safety. He was taking her to safety.

She tried to rationalize that explanation, but considering the thickening canopy of trees overhead and the mushy ground beneath their feet, she couldn't reconcile the two. He wasn't from here…didn't understand the danger.

Bears…wolves…snakes…not to mention quicksand.

The swamp was many things, but safe didn't rate high on that list.

Then she heard it.

The squish of waterlogged soil behind them. The brush of foliage against man-made fabric to the far right. Her head jerked left as a twig snapped in that direction.

Fear hijacked her courage and sent the sting of adrenaline soaring through her veins.

Cops?

That was her first thought. Maybe they thought she and Aidan were Lester and…

No.

Not cops.

Whoever had fanned out around them were not the good guys.

Evil.

Not Lester, either. He'd only come back here to see after his interests...the children.

She ran faster, staying right on Aidan's heels.

She smelled the water before he stalled on the bank.

The odor of decaying fish and foliage was stronger the closer they got.

He yanked her against his chest and whispered in her ear. "We're going into the water. Try not to make any more sound than necessary. They may have night vision and thermal imaging. We don't need to give them any other ammunition."

Everything he'd said after water was lost on her.

They couldn't go into the water.

It teemed with nature's handiwork...with danger.

As if reading her mind, he shoved the gun into his waistband at the small of his back and lifted her off her feet. She bit down on her lower lip to stem a gasp. He brought her against his chest and started forward.

She felt him descending into the water but incredibly he made no sound.

How could he do that?

In less than a minute, she felt the cold liquid swishing against her bottom. He was waist-deep in the water and moving forward without the slightest sound.

Despite the physical exertion required to carry her one-hundred-ten pound frame and trudge through water at that depth his respiration was slow, even. His heartbeat strong and steady. It didn't flutter like hers. She stared at the handsome face only inches from hers. A new kind of trepidation trickled through her.

Who was this man?

A dozen little things flashed through her mind.

The way he could practically read her mind. The way he moved…soundless, fluid. He was one with the water. One with the night.

Those silly ideas about vampires and such attempted to edge into her ruminating but she banished them.

He stilled, held her tight against him.

She heard nothing. Sensed nothing. Only the roar of blood in her ears, the desperate hammering of her heart.

He started moving forward again.

The water deepened.

She shivered as the cold enveloped her almost to her neck. The water was really deep here.

He stopped again.

This time, he tilted his head down and whispered into her ear. "How long can you hold your breath?"

Panic flared like fireworks on the Fourth of July. She wanted to rant at him. Was he kidding? Instead, she forced the trembling in her body to cease. She had to be strong. He would have a good reason for asking the question.

She lifted her mouth to his ear. "I'm not sure. A minute, maybe." God, could she hold it that long? She'd never timed herself. She had no idea.

"They're very close," he murmured. "Four, possibly five. I don't want to risk those odds."

"You're sure it's not the police?" She stared into his eyes as best she could in the near total darkness, praying it was a possibility.

He moved his head slowly up and down.

His attention jerked back toward the woods behind her.

Whatever he'd heard, it must have been close because she felt the tension radiate through his strong body.

His gaze moved back down to hers and he took a deep breath.

Her eyes rounded with terror, but somehow she managed to drag in a gulp of air before he plunged beneath the water.

Aidan opened his eyes and watched her through the dark shroud of water. In moments, his vision had adjusted fully. She was afraid. She felt stiff in his arms. They needed to stay under as long as possible.

Galen's men were close.

He needed them to survey this area, deem it clear and move on.

He'd known when he saw the bullet hole in the back of the cop's head that this wasn't Jerry Lester's work. Galen had counted on her being drawn back here.

Her eyes suddenly opened wide with fear. She struggled in his hold but he held her tighter, reached out to her with his mind. *Relax. Trust me.*

Galen's men were on the bank now, directly overhead. Though muffled, the amplified sounds of their approach reached Aidan's ears well ahead of them.

Darby jerked, almost breaking free of his hold.

He pulled her hard against him. And then she did the one thing that there was no turning back from. She exhaled. He watched the bubbles move upward, break the surface.

He froze, braced for attack.

Nothing.

She struggled to free herself once more.

A sound vibrated from above, as if the enemy was once more on the move.

A few more seconds—that's all he needed. But she wasn't going to make it a few more seconds.

He held her tightly against him and closed his mouth over hers, used his tongue to pry her lips apart and forced the last breath he possessed into her lungs.

Even as his brain rebelled against his action, his body reacted to kissing her. The sensations devoured him like a raging lion, dragging him deeper and deeper into that place of pure need.

She stopped fighting him, fisted her fingers in his shirt and flattened her chest against his chest.

He surged upward, breaking the surface of the water without breaking the kiss.

She pulled free, gasped for air.

His struggles to draw in a breath matched hers. He'd almost waited too long.

He listened beyond her frantic gasps, be-yond the uncharacteristic pounding in his chest. The enemy had moved farther north, forty or fifty meters.

Altering their course, he started back the way they had come.

She laid her cheek against his chest, her heart still fluttering like a captured bird. Her body trembled uncontrollably from the cold. He wanted to sit down on the bank and hold her in such a way to comfort her, but he couldn't take that risk.

He pushed forward, all the while keeping his senses finely attuned to their surroundings.

A fork in the waterway presented an additional layer of separation. Instead of continuing in the direction they'd come, he took the other. Galen would expect them to attempt to make it back to the boat.

Aidan smiled. He didn't need the boat.

He could walk all night and then some.

His training included sensory shutdown. He could go on and on without feeling pain or exhaustion if he chose. The price would be high for a short time afterwards, but he could do it…would do it if necessary.

DARBY DIDN'T KNOW how much time had passed. It felt like hours. Had to have been hours.

Aidan just kept walking with her in his arms. He had to be exhausted.

"Wait," she whispered, still afraid to speak out loud.

He stopped and looked down at her, his movements mechanical.

"Yes."

"I can walk now." She scrambled out of his arms. It wasn't as if she would get any wetter. At least she'd stopped shaking. He'd been walking through waist-deep water for…for hours. Again, the idea that he possessed that kind of stamina amazed her.

"We should keep moving," he suggested. His tone sounded strangely emotionless.

She tried not to let it get to her. Her nerves were already far too raw with fear.

Her so-called gift had failed her. Here they were, lost in the swamp without any idea which way to go. She hadn't heard the voices…the children…for hours. Not since those men had come after them.

Your life is in grave danger.

The men in the white coats…she said you would understand.

She stumbled but caught herself as the voice echoed inside her brain. Could those men after them back there have been…

Who else could it be if it wasn't Jerry Lester, and it definitely wasn't. She knew that with complete certainty.

And it wasn't the police…surely they would have called out to them, warned that the police were in pursuit.

She'd dreamed about the men in the white coats all her life.

It had to be them.

She glanced at the silent man at her side.

Could he possibly have any idea just how bad this was?

Yes.

She blinked. Startled by the answer that echoed in her skull.

Of course he knew. That's why he'd almost drowned them both back there in an attempt to keep them safe.

"I'm sorry," she said quietly, still a little afraid of being overhead. For all she knew, Lester could be lurking around the next bend in the waterway.

Aidan paused, looked down at her. "Why are you sorry?"

She turned her hands palms up. "For dragging you into this mess. I'm sure you had no idea what this was going to turn into when you were assigned to support this case."

Even in the dark, she could see the energy burning in those dark eyes. "No apology is necessary. I'm here because it's my job."

He started forward again but she just stood there staring at his broad back.

He was here because it was his job?

She stormed after him as best she could in water up to her belly button. The drag of the water slowed her dramatic display of outrage considerably. She grabbed him by the arm and turned him around. Which would have been impossible had he not allowed her to do so.

"I guess that aqua erotic kiss back there was your job, too?"

He looked confused for about two seconds. "No," he admitted. "It was about self-indulgence. But necessary to survival."

She told herself that his admission was a compliment, while a tiny part of her still wondered about his sudden mechanical actions, his monotone. "I guess I can accept that," she allowed when he continued to look at her as if he expected a response.

She sloshed forward with renewed determination. She didn't know where the hell they were going or why they were still walking through the water. But then, she was no FBI agent. He surely had some plan…some reason.

"You wished for a different explanation?"

She faced him once more. "What?" Confusion joined the other barrage of emotions churning inside her.

"You wanted me to provide an explanation different from the one I gave you."

How could he do that? Know what she was thinking.

Well, if he already knew what she was thinking, she might as well just say what she *really* thought.

"Actually," she braced her hands on her hips, "I was hoping you'd say you kissed me because you just couldn't resist locking your lips with mine. Or that you were so completely captivated by my beauty beneath the murky swamp water that you just couldn't stop yourself."

His fingers were in her hair before the words stopped echoing around them. He kissed her hard, his mouth unyielding, promising whatever she was willing to accept. She melted against him, felt every incredibly hard ridge and contour. His body was magnificent. When she thought about the fact that this man had carried her for hours...had given her the very breath from his lips to keep her safe...she wanted to weep. Instead, she kissed him back.

He pulled away all too soon, his breath surprisingly uneven. Her heart stumbled at the realization that she'd actually gotten to him this time. Shaken him.

"We have to keep moving," he murmured against her lips.

She nodded.

He started forward once more and she followed, thoroughly contented. A smile lifted the corners of her mouth. They had something here...something special. It wasn't just his job.

The light that exploded in her frontal lobe caught her completely off guard. She grabbed her head in her hands and doubled over with the intensity of it.

Take us home.

She straightened, the breath whooshing out of her lungs.

The children.

Please...take us home.

She turned around in the water, tried to see through the dark.

Where?

Aidan was watching her. Worried.

"They're here," she murmured. *They're here…somewhere.*

Here.

So close.

She surged forward, moving past Aidan. He followed, giving her space. Somehow understanding.

"I'm coming," she muttered.

Darby pushed through the water, not caring how much noise she made. She was getting closer. Almost there.

She stumbled. Fell face-first into the water this time.

Dammit.

She grappled to catch herself, flailed her arms, grabbed for something—anything—but it was no use. She went down. She scrambled onto the bank at the same time that Aidan's arms went around her waist.

He seemed to be moving slower now.

But who wouldn't.

"I've gotta get out of this water," she said, exhausted. She clawed at the bank to pull herself upward. Her fingers wrapped around something hard—a root or stick.

It glowed eerily white against the grays and browns of the bank.

Long, thin.

A…bone.

Before the scream could escape her throat, Aidan had turned her away from the horrific sight and pulled her to him.

Her anguish was muffled against his chest.

Take us home.

Chapter Ten

Spotlights pierced the night.

The sound of radios crackling, a helicopter flying overhead and crime scene investigators wading through the muck created an unnatural cacophony amid the wild swamp setting.

Light and shadow bounced off each other, filtering through the heavy moss and highlighting gnarled cypress. The glassy surface of the water stood eerily still, holding its secrets unseen within its black depths.

Aidan shut out the noise and scene developing around the discovery of skeletal remains and focused on the dark unmoving silence beyond. Galen's men were somewhere in this swamp. Perhaps Galen himself. A rush of knowing went through him. Yes. Galen was here. Watching, waiting for an opportunity to strike.

It didn't surprise Aidan that he'd found himself new followers. A man like that could always sway support for his cause. Nothing short of death would stop him.

Aidan felt no qualms about delivering that ultimate fate. The man meant nothing to him. That he was the creative mind behind who and what Aidan was carried no weight. His gaze shifted to Eve—Darby—where Detective Willis and his partner were grilling her about how she came to be here.

Moving closer, Aidan monitored the conversation for questions about him. Darby would not think to mention that he had introduced himself as an agent for the FBI. Willis's men had already likely told him that she had a friend accompanying her now. It wasn't unusual for a woman to have a male friend. Willis wouldn't ask. Not now. He was too focused on the discovery. Praying it would be the remains he sought so that he could put another aspect of this case to rest.

But there was still Jerry Lester.

Aidan slowly surveyed the shadowy woods around their location. He was out there. Not so far away. Aidan could feel his presence. He wanted to watch Willis's men struggle with what he'd had to abandon in order to remain free. He wanted to watch Darby Shepard. She was his new obsession.

Maybe because she was a teacher or maybe because she'd touched his mind. Aidan couldn't be sure. His mind was twisted...unreliable.

"I should haul you in for even being out here," Willis threatened Darby. "I've got one man dead and another one missing." He glanced at Aidan but said nothing about him. Though his dislike carried across the night, made Aidan curious.

Perhaps it was that the detective didn't like strangers. Or maybe he sensed Aidan's knowledge of this case and didn't like anyone horning in on his territory. Then again, it could be Darby. Aidan noted the way the detective touched her...looked at her. He'd ensured that one of his men brought a blanket to put around her.

Aidan stayed on the edge of the fray, not wanting to draw unnecessary attention to himself and needing the distance for focus on the threat that lay beyond the events evolving here. Alerting the authorities had been simple since his cellular phone was waterproof and operated via satellite.

The first hint of dawn had lightened the

sky. The coming sunrise would be a welcome benefit to the investigators scouring the scene. But for Aidan, it would present additional problems. In the dark, he maintained the advantage. He didn't want Darby to be a sitting duck when the sun broke through the trees. He wanted her out of here before then.

"I had to come," Darby argued with the detective. Her gaze wandered toward the place where she'd made her gruesome discovery.

"Sir, we've got trouble."

Willis turned to the officer who'd just spoken. "What the hell is it now?" He slapped at a mosquito that lit on his neck.

The officer leaned close to his boss and whispered, "Two reporters have managed to find their way back here."

Willis swore hotly, repeatedly. "Get her out of here," he growled, then tossed a look at Aidan. "Him, too. I don't want those reporters getting a whiff of her involvement."

Two officers escorted Darby and Aidan farther down the waterway to an area where it widened enough for a properly equipped helicopter to land on the water's surface. Any other landing would have been impossible in the dense woods.

When one of the officers would have led

Darby into the water, Aidan reached out and pulled her back to him. He lifted her into his arms before she could question the move and carried her to the transport vehicle.

Inside, they settled in the cargo area of the craft and braced for ascension.

When they'd cleared the treetops, leaving the dangers of the swamp behind, Darby looked up at him, her expression grim. "He's still out there. They're not going to find him."

She was right.

Detective Willis would not find the serial killer Jerry Lester today or even tomorrow.

But the children were safe now.

"Whether they find him or not doesn't matter." He put his arm around her and pulled her close. "He can't touch you now."

DARBY PRESSED her forehead against the cool tile and allowed the hot water to pummel her flesh for a long time after she'd cleansed the river water and swamp mud from her body. She was so cold. Even the blanket or Aidan's closeness on the journey home couldn't ease the chill that came from within.

She didn't have to wait for official confirmation of what she'd found. She knew the remains belonged to the missing children.

Victims of that monster Jerry Lester. She scrubbed the water from her face and tried to understand the vibes she'd picked up those last few hours in the swamp.

He'd been there, she'd felt him. Sensed his sick presence all around her. At first, she'd thought it was only because of the…remains. That maybe she was picking up on his presence as connected to when he'd buried them there. But that wasn't the case. He'd been in that swamp somewhere, not so far away, watching.

He wanted to see. Wanted to observe her discovering his buried treasure. He'd kept them to himself all this time; now he wanted the world to know that he had spoken the truth. Not that he'd had a lot of choice. The police were on to him. He couldn't protect his secrets any longer. Apparently some had doubted his claims regarding other work. They had thought it was a mere ploy to escape the death penalty.

But he hadn't lied and he wouldn't escape.

He was going to die…slowly…painfully. She couldn't see more than that, couldn't see that, really. She felt it, though—felt it with complete certainty. Aidan knew, too, somehow.

Every time she thought she understood a

little something about Aidan, he went and threw her off balance again. She'd gotten used to the way he seemed to be able to read her thoughts. Then he'd started to sense other things at the same time she did.

Too bizarre.

An image of men in white coats flashed through her mind. They had been in that swamp, too. Maybe not the guys in the white coats, but men they had sent to find her.

What did they want?

As soon as she got past one threat, something else popped up. What was with this sudden let's-get-Darby trend?

She shut off the water and stood there, unmoving for a long moment. No. That wasn't true. The men in the white coats had always loomed over her life. They just hadn't known she was here until now.

She'd played quiet mouse all these years and stayed safe. Now, in the course of a few days, she'd been exposed to the danger that had always been there deep in the shadows of a past she couldn't remember.

As foolish as she knew it was, a part of her felt as if Aidan understood. He knew, maybe simply sensed, that there was more for her to worry about than Jerry Lester.

Not once in her life had she felt as connected to another human being as she did to Aidan. It went way beyond the physical…beyond mere attraction.

She thought of that hollow feeling that had always haunted her. As if some part of herself was missing. She'd wondered if perhaps she'd been a twin and her sibling had been lost early on in pregnancy. She'd read about it. One in eight pregnancies started out as twins, she remembered.

But this connection she and Aidan shared, although every bit as intense, was not the brotherly-sisterly kind. This was the man-woman kind. The me-Tarzan-you-Jane kind.

Her life was a wreck.

She was supposed to start her new job today and look at her. She pulled the towel from its bar and swabbed her body dry.

Two police officers were stationed in her courtyard, one near the elevator on this very floor. She knew Willis hoped Lester would come after her, especially considering she'd tipped his hand and led the police to his one ace in the hole. But he hadn't minded that she'd done that. He'd enjoyed the show. Reveled in the attention to his work.

Willis needn't worry.

Jerry Lester was never leaving that swamp.

She had no explanation for her conclusion, only that she felt it with utter certainty.

After she'd dried her hair and slathered on some lotion, she pulled on her terry cloth robe. It felt good. She glanced at her lucky sweater lying on the foot of the bed. Why on earth had she bothered digging out that old thing? She'd worn it at home all the time during her high school years. When she studied…when she worried…most of the time, she admitted. She'd even taken it to college with her. But after her parents' death, she'd had no use for it.

Luck had failed her.

Maybe all the painful things she'd experienced lately had subconsciously made her long for the old ratty garment. She picked it up and smelled the fabric. It smelled like home… like her room…like the past. Maybe some part of her had just felt compelled to reach out for comforting mementos of the past.

She should go home more often. The time she and Aidan had spent looking through old family photo albums had soothed her, made her feel connected to her parents once more. She'd needed that.

As she brushed her long hair she thought

of something else she desperately needed right now.

Him.

She had no intention of pretending anymore. The memory of him holding her beneath that water…giving her his last breath. If those men had found them, would they even be alive right now?

Not for another moment was she going to sit on the sidelines and wait for life to happen to her. She was going to make it happen. If she could mentally track a serial killer, she could damn sure have an intimate relationship with a man she was fiercely attracted to.

When she moved into the living room it was semidark. The curtains drawn tight, allowing only a narrow shaft of light here and there where they didn't completely meet. Shadows and light played around the room, reminding her all too much of last night's journey into the depths of nature's primordial world. She scratched the back of Wiz's head as she passed the sofa. She'd filled his food and water bowls and changed his litter box after letting him in this morning. Obviously she wasn't the only one who'd spent the night prowling around.

Her breath caught as the door to her apartment opened. She relaxed when Aidan stepped inside. He'd apparently gone to his own place across the hall to shower.

Heat infused her as her gaze paused first on his bare chest where that trademark black shirt lay open. Clean black trousers had replaced the ones he'd ruined in the murky swamp. And his feet were bare. She smiled, suddenly fascinated by the shape and length of those masculine feet.

"You need sleep," he said, that deep voice rougher than usual. The sound rasped over her nerve endings, made her shiver. "I'll keep watch."

She moved closer to him, reveled in watching him watch her. "And what about you? Don't you need sleep as well?" She thought about the way he'd carried her through that swamp for hours. His strength was incredible, unending. How was it possible to have such physical endurance? Maybe it wasn't. Maybe she'd imagined the whole night. Then she remembered the way he'd kissed her beneath that dark water. The way he'd held her close to his chest, close to his heart, while he trudged through that swamp. Need shuddered through her. He was truly incredible.

Another memory bobbed to the surface. The way he'd been afterward—mechanical…autonomic. Even his voice, the cadence of his speech, had been different. Just how much of himself had he been forced to shut down to go above and beyond normal physical limitations?

"You must be exhausted," she suggested. It wasn't a question. He had to be. No normal human could have done what he did and not be totally wiped out.

"I'll be fine. You should sleep."

That handsome face was carefully schooled to a neutral expression. He didn't want her to know… wouldn't let her see what he really felt.

She moved another step closer. "I don't want to sleep."

"When the adrenaline wears off, you'll want to sleep," he countered.

She took a position less than a foot away from him and tilted her head back to look at him. "What do you suggest I do until then?"

He licked those sexy lips and opened that amazing mouth to make some response but words, apparently, failed him.

"Kiss me, Aidan," she murmured. "Kiss me like you did when you were trying to save my life."

Long, slender fingers cupped her face. Artist's fingers, she mused. But so strong, so skilled in far more things than she knew. As those sensual lips descended to meet hers, one thought rose above all others.

Secrets.

This man had many, many secrets.

His mouth moved slowly at first, savoring, teasing, softly, tenderly, as if he had forever or wanted desperately to memorize every detail of her taste.

She stopped thinking, lost herself in his kiss. His lips were firm and yet soft at the same time. He controlled the pressure, the depth of the kiss.

But she wanted more.

Her arms went up to his shoulders. She pushed the shirt away and smoothed her palms over his wondrously sculpted torso. Flames roared through her, igniting every part of her as she felt the smoothness of his skin, the hardness of male muscle covered in sleek satin. Up and over that sensual landscape her fingers reached until they found a home in his silky hair. And then she traced the planes and angles of his face.

As good as his kiss felt, she had to see. She pulled away to allow her mind the added stimuli of seeing what her fingers felt.

He stood very still as she learned his lips with the tips of her fingers…felt the heat and softness. The squareness of his jaw, the lean planes of his cheeks. High cheekbones, the slender bridge of his nose. A strong brow, un-lined by age. He couldn't be much older than her.

Her heart bumped against her sternum with each frantic beat, with each shallow breath. She couldn't get enough air into her lungs, couldn't stop touching him. She wanted to know every part of him.

He lifted his hands to her face and touched her the same way. His own respiration grew rapid and shallow, a perfect match to hers. He pulled a handful of her hair to his face and inhaled deeply, closed those glittering dark eyes as if that were very nearly more than he could bear.

She tugged free the sash to her robe and shrugged out of it, allowing it to fall to the floor in a half circle around her feet. His eyes opened and that impassioned gaze traveled down the length of her and back, then settled on her eyes.

"You are so beautiful."

He turned her around and pulled her back against him, held her that way, with his arms cradled around her waist and his chin against her hair until she could no longer bear the friction of his trousers against her bare bottom, the feel of his hardened sex restrained behind the fabric.

As if reading her mind or sensing her need, he drew back a few inches and kissed her naked shoulder. Slowly, he kissed his way down her back, moving her long hair aside as he went. When he reached the curve of her hip, he knelt, his hands bracketing her waist. He kissed her hip, then lower, until he reached the next curve where her bottom met her thigh. Then he turned her around.

The image of him kneeling before her took her breath away. His gaze never leaving hers, he leaned forward and pressed a kiss next to her belly button. Her entire body quivered in response.

His fingers glided over her skin, the caress so light she wasn't even certain he actually touched her though she watched his every move. Downward, tracing the shapes of her legs only to make their way along her inner thighs, those long masculine fingers set every inch of her on fire.

He kissed his way up her rib cage until he encountered her breasts. He pressed his face between them, the feel of his breath on her skin fueling the frenzy already out of control inside her. This was too much. She couldn't catch her breath, couldn't wait any longer.

She gasped when he stood, towered above her. Before she could think of what he intended, he swept her into his arms and carried her to the kitchen. He sat her on the counter next to the fridge. Another gasp slipped past her lips at the cold feel of tile beneath her bottom. She shivered…started to ask what he was doing, but his focused movements overwhelmed her ability to speak.

Leaving her sitting there, he fumbled in the freezer compartment, then came back to her with a handful of ice cubes. He dropped them on the counter. Something intensely carnal surged inside her as the cubes slid this way and that.

There was something primal in his eyes… something savage. She sucked in a sharp breath at the ferocity of it.

He picked up one of the ice cubes and touched her. She caught her breath. With slow, aching precision, he made a path down her chest, over her breast and around her nipple. Her eyes closed. She pressed her head back against the cabinet, her fingers clutching at the counter on either side of her. He licked at the water left behind by the ice. Suckled at her breast.

She had to touch him…couldn't resist. Her fingers threaded into his hair as he alternately cooled her flesh with the ice and set her aflame with his mouth. She whimpered and moaned, begging without words for him to stop torturing her. But he was relentless. He would not stop touching her, tasting her, tantalizing her skin with the fire and ice.

His mouth moved lower, closer to the part of her throbbing for his attention. He hadn't even touched her there and she felt ready to explode.

Images filtered through her mind—the two of them, their bodies connected in the most intimate of ways. Him plunging into her, her rising to meet his every thrust. He filled her so completely, over and over again.

Orgasm came in an unexpected rush.

She screamed his name.

He was there. Not the fantasy…the real thing. Kissing her, whispering sweet words to her. Just envisioning making love with him had made her come. How would she ever bear the real thing?

She felt herself being lifted, felt him crush her against his chest as he carried her. She couldn't make her eyes open, even when he lowered her onto the bed.

She reached for him, but he was no longer there. Her eyes opened, searched the nearly dark room. The sound of fabric sliding over skin drew her attention to the foot of the bed. He straightened, tossed aside his trousers and briefs.

He was magnificent. Perfect. Every powerful muscle defined so beautifully. Her eyes marveled in the strength of his masculine body, in the generous size of his sex.

Like a sleek panther about to close in on its prey, he climbed onto the end of the bed, moved onto all fours, that glittering dark gaze focused intently on her.

Trembling like a lamb about to be presented up for slaughter, she reached out to him...needed to make the connection complete.

He drew back slightly, just out of her reach.

She scrambled onto all fours, matching his dominant stance, ready to fight for what she wanted. They watched each other warily for a few moments, then he made the first move.

He twined his fingers in her hair and pulled her closer. She turned her head when he would have claimed her mouth.

Her heart thundered, her mind whirled with confusion. He wanted her...she wanted him. But she didn't understand why he didn't take her completely, or why she taunted him. She simply could not help herself.

He pressed his lips to her ear and whispered roughly, "Are you sure this is what you want?"

She turned her face to his. "Yes. Aren't you?"

He wanted her. She knew he did.

He cradled her face in his hands and drew her mouth closer to his. But instead of kissing her, he murmured, "I've never stopped wanting you."

She nipped at his lips with her teeth. "Then take me. I'm yours."

"You've always been mine."

His mouth closed over hers and the confusion and uncertainty melted away. He lowered her onto the bed, coming down on top of her. Her legs went around his as his weight settled against her. The slightly rougher feel of his, dusted with masculine hair, made her giddy.

It felt more right than anything she'd ever experienced. They belonged together. The intimate knowledge settled over her, inside her.

His fingers entwined with hers, he nudged her and she spread her legs wider in invitation. Her whole being yearned for him... needed only him. He stared deeply into her eyes as he pushed slowly inside her. The resistance he met gave him pause, he hesitated. But she urged him on, wriggling her hips and trying to open wider.

He kissed her—long and slow—until she relaxed so completely that she couldn't think of anything else but his lips moving on hers, his tongue teasing hers.

He pushed deeper inside and she came again even as he made the seal complete, filling her to capacity and then some. He drank in the sounds of her release as if it were an intoxicating brew, held her hands tighter, pressed his hips more firmly into hers, absorbing ripple after ripple of her pleasure.

She didn't know how many minutes had passed with him kissing her mouth, her face, her throat. She might have blacked out...still couldn't catch her breath. He moved his hips only a little, as if he feared hurting her.

He was holding back, allowing her to enjoy all the pleasure while he restrained himself. She pulled her hands free of his and pushed against his chest.

"Turn over," she demanded, a new kind of determination charging through her. This wasn't supposed to be one-sided.

He paused in his ministrations. His eyes were slightly glazed but not nearly enough. He was still hanging on to control.

"Turn over," she ordered, pushing harder against his chest.

He rolled onto his back, pulling her with him. She bit back a wince when the position sent him deeper inside her. He was so damn big. His hands were on her waist instantly, lifting her just enough to ease the pressure. She pushed those masterful hands away and scolded, "It's my turn now."

He curled his arms around the pillow under his head and lay very still. Well, she'd just see how long that relaxed pose lasted.

Aidan fisted his fingers into the pillow and clenched his teeth together to resist the impulse to lift his hips. His body pulsed with need. He wanted to tuck her back under him and drive into her until he howled with release. But he couldn't. She was too small.

He'd already caused her discomfort. He closed his eyes and fought to control the desire roaring through his body. He wouldn't hurt her again.

She started to move and a groan wrenched from his throat. She moved slowly, sinuously at first. He could feel the tension in her body caused by the continued discomfort…yet she wanted this.

He found himself mesmerized by her movements. Her eyes closed, her back arched slightly, her long hair trailed over her shoulders and down her back, making him crazy with want. She rode him slow and easy, her tight walls dragging along his length, making him want to cry out with the incredible pleasure of it.

Up and down, squeezing, tugging. He wouldn't survive this. Couldn't take it…no amount of training could have prepared him for the devouring heat…the overwhelming sensations.

She rocked a little faster, pumping him with a rhythm that fired his blood. The thrust of her breasts made him hunger to taste them again. He reached for her but she pushed his hands away, wouldn't let him touch her. She was fighting another plunge toward orgasm, panting, making small guttural sounds with the effort of keeping up the pace when she wanted to let go.

The first wave of completion swept over him and he lost it.

"No more," he rasped. He had to finish this.

He rolled her beneath him and plunged into her tight, rippling body. She came around him, the contractions sending him completely over his own edge. He thrust deep, hard, over and over. His entire body spasmed, then relaxed, again and again as the single purest form of pleasure he'd ever experienced flooded his senses. He pumped once, twice more, milking the last of his seed from his body.

His eyes opened, settled on her angelic face.

She was his. Nothing short of his own death would take her from him.

He would protect her from the very men who had created her for him.

Chapter Eleven

French Quarter
Unspecified Location

His creations were spectacular.

Even equipped with night vision and every other advantage imaginable, his men had failed to capture the two seers.

Galen had watched the thermal imaging scan as the mission played out. The male had simply disappeared into thin air, along with the female.

But they had been there, right under the noses of his men.

Impossible, his team leader had exclaimed. Body heat, wherever they had hidden, would have been picked up by the scan. There had to have been an underground escape route, he had insisted.

But Galen had surveyed the location personally, had walked the area, ending up right back where he'd started without an answer. Then he'd known. He'd crouched down on the bank and dipped his hand into the water. Even now, he had to smile at the ingenuity of the male's strategy.

The water.

The seers had hidden beneath the murky surface of the water. At this time of year, the temperature was certainly cool enough to drop body temperature beneath the scan's search setting.

Each of the Enforcers was a phenomenon in his own right. Whatever gene manipulation man attempted, each human was individual and the result varied. Therefore, each one created had evolved with his own special skill set. All were physically and mentally superior to the rest of mankind. But he had to admit that the one called Aidan amazed him with his gift of elevated sensory perceptions. The female could be every bit as good; she merely lacked the essential training.

What a magnificent pair they would make. He wondered what kind of offspring they would produce. There was no precedent for breeding among the Enforcers, though he suspected the country's esteemed leader would produce the first. Still, the superior genes of the original Enforcer Cain would be diluted by her lesser genetic code. Galen was not interested in that avenue.

He wanted perfection. Aidan appeared as close to perfect as could be achieved with current technology and without converting to machine augmentation. The seer was both beautiful and powerful. His strength surprised even Galen. His intelligence level dazzled. He would not be easy to capture. And yet, he was capable of being distracted.

His growing obsession with the female—the one who had been created to be his mate—was proof positive. Galen smiled. He would lay odds that Aidan had no idea that the only reason a female had been designed was for future breeding potential. Special training and intensive bonding sessions had been included in their early education. The female, of course, would not remember those sessions since she had been deemed a failure and her memory wiped. He imagined that even if she remembered parts of her training, there would be skips in her logic since she had worked so hard against her teachers.

Somehow, she had realized that failure to

cooperate was her ticket to freedom. Galen turned that concept over in his mind. How could she have known that freedom existed in any capacity outside Center's walls?

Like any scientist, he had encountered instances where unexplainable knowledge or recall had been excused by the theory of genetic memories. How did an individual born and living in contemporary times recall vividly the exact details of an incident that occurred hundreds of years prior?

Galen gave no credence to such occurrences. However, that this female seer could have known that a world outside Center existed before her training had exposed her to that data defied any other explanation.

That issue might very well remain a mystery. The matter did not particularly concern him. He had only one priority at this point—capturing the two seers.

The Collective and Center had taken everything from him…had left him with nothing. He could envision no way to regain his former status and certainly would never be able to reassemble the Concern, the new organization he had secretly built after being shunned by the Collective and Center. He was on his own.

At the very least, he could start his new

venture with his two greatest creations. The male would fight him, try to eliminate him. But Galen knew his one weakness now. He would exploit that.

And the female. Well, her containment would be a simple matter. She had many weaknesses. But he would see that she received the proper training to alleviate those inadequacies. Already he had set the plan in motion.

Soon she would realize she really had no choice in the matter. He wasn't worried about Center's involvement. He felt certain the male would not want to risk her elimination, which would most certainly be ordered in light of what Galen suspected. He wondered what Darby Shepard would think if she discovered that her hero—her lover—had been sent to determine whether or not she should continue to exist.

Very soon he would know all he wanted to about her.

Already he'd left her a gift.

Château Garden Apartments
Garden District

AIDAN SURVEYED the headlines of the *Times-Picayune,* as well as several other local newspapers, to see what had been reported about the discovery near Lester's swamp habitat.

As he perused the numerous articles that related much and verified little, he also listened to the conversation between Darby and the Shepard family attorney, Mr. Thomas. She'd called his office and he'd agreed to come by this evening.

"I'm sorry I can't help you, Darby," Thomas was saying. "Your father handled the adoption personally. The only thing I did was review the contract for him. I had my reservations, as any attorney would, about that kind of private, closed adoption, but it worked out, didn't it?" He smiled warmly at Darby.

She managed a faint smile in return. "Yes, sir, it did. I guess I was just curious." She sighed wistfully. "After all this time, I don't suppose it really matters." She leveled a hopeful look on the older man. "Did you keep a copy of the contract at your office?"

"I didn't." He shrugged. "It was a personal venture so I didn't bother keeping a copy. Surely your father kept the original."

"I couldn't find anything even remotely related to my adoption."

"I wish I could do more, but unfortunately I don't know much of anything about it." Mr.

Thomas pushed to his feet. "Please don't hesitate to call me in the future, my dear." He patted her on the back as she walked with him to the door. "I assure you I'm generally a good deal more useful than this."

Darby laughed, the sound pleasing to the ear but hollow. "I appreciate you stopping by."

The attorney gave her a fatherly hug. "Call me again soon. Don't let so much time pass next time." He glanced in Aidan's direction. "Good to meet you, Agent Tanner."

Aidan nodded. Every instinct told him that the other shoe was about to drop.

Thomas hesitated when he would have gone out the door, a frown furrowed his brow. "There was one thing," he said to Darby. He shook his head then, disgusted with the effects of aging. "I'd almost forgotten."

Tension vibrated through Aidan, but he kept his gaze focused on the newspapers spread in front of him on the dining table.

"Anything you remember might prove useful," Darby urged, her tone hopeful.

Aidan could feel her holding her breath. She wanted to know the details of her past, now more so than before.

Even in the short time that he had known

her, he'd sensed the restlessness growing inside her. It was easy to see that as soon as the business with Lester was over, she would focus more fully on learning the truth about where she'd come from. Though he doubted any real success would come of her enthusiasm, the Collective, O'Riley in particular, would not see it from that prospective. They would only see what they wanted to see, which was a confirmed risk.

Her elimination would be ordered.

No margin for error.

Aidan couldn't let that happen.

His jaw hardened and his hands clenched into fists.

He had to find a way to protect her from Galen as well as the Collective. She was a part of him. Despite the gaps in his memory of their time together, he sensed how close they had been. Knew on some level that they had been created for each other. Now that connection was complete on a physical level. The mental connection grew more solid with each passing hour. He'd sealed his fate when he'd made her his this morning. That intimate bonding had completed him in a way that left no doubt as to what he must do.

He would not allow her to be harmed...no matter the price.

"There was a gentleman your father dealt with," Thomas said as he stroked his chin thoughtfully. "An Irish name, as I recall. O'Riley." He nodded, his eyes narrowing as he rolled the name around in his mind. "Yes. Richard O'Riley. But he was only the courier. Your father never dealt directly with your biological parents." He chuckled. "I'd completely forgotten that name." With a shrug he added, "They say memory is the first thing to go."

Darby tiptoed and kissed his cheek. "Thank you so much for your help."

Aidan returned his attention to the newspapers as she promised to keep in touch and closed and locked the door behind her departing visitor. That she now knew O'Riley's name was a serious breach of security. Even he couldn't ignore that, despite how badly he wanted to. What he couldn't understand was why O'Riley would have used his real name. It didn't make sense. The infraction actually started with him. Aidan certainly wouldn't need to point out that error in judgment. O'Riley would know and that knowledge might very well cost both Darby and her old friend Mr. Thomas their lives.

Darby considered the information Howard Thomas had relayed as she locked the door behind him. *Richard O'Riley.* Oddly the name sounded familiar. She didn't see how it could, but maybe she'd heard her father say it at some point in her life. Though she doubted that. He and her mother never, ever spoke of her life before or of the adoption. She had assumed it pained them to be reminded that she was not biologically their child. But it shouldn't have because she couldn't have loved them more.

As far as she was concerned, her biological parents were nothing more than the sperm and egg donors. Her only reason for looking into her past was the fear of the "men in white coats" that loomed over her life.

She wanted to put that anxiety to rest.

A smile stretched across her mouth and those troubling thoughts vanished when her gaze settled on Aidan. She did so love to look at him. A rush of heat surged through her as her mind replayed their lovemaking. Nothing she had ever experienced had even come close to making her feel so alive. He completed her in a way that still boggled her mind. She knew almost nothing about him and yet she trusted him with every fiber of her being.

He was her soul mate.

She hadn't really believed in soul mates before. At least, not one for her. It wasn't that she'd been unpopular in high school or college or even in the past four years as an independent, wage-earning single woman. She just hadn't made herself available, she supposed. Reserved and selective defined her attitude toward the opposite sex for the most part. Though, in reality, the whole reserved-selective thing was more about being shy. Her old schoolmates would laugh if they heard that. Darby Shepard was not afraid of anything, they would insist. She represented the only one of their group who would walk through a cemetery at night all alone and not suffer the slightest twinge of discomfort, much less fright.

Fearless, determined—those were the words her friends had used to describe her as they'd autographed one another's school yearbooks.

Fear hadn't really had anything to do with her shyness with boys and men, she now knew. It was more about patience and the subconscious sense of certainty that the right man would come along.

And now he had.

She felt, without reservation, that Aidan was the only man for her. She shivered as memories of his kisses, of his plunging deep inside her, invaded her mental discussion with herself. No way would sex ever be that right with anyone else. She almost shook her head, but resisted the impulse since he might notice. Not just sex. Lovemaking. They'd made love.

"There is no mention of you in any of the articles related to...what happened," he said, breaking into her thoughts. The mere sound of his voice washed over her like a soothing balm, made her yearn to feel his arms around her again.

"Detective Willis assured me he would keep my name out of the case from now on." She was glad he'd lived up to his promise.

"According to the *Times-Picayune,* it will be a while before the identities of the remains are confirmed."

Darby thought of the parents and how they would have to wait longer still to know...but she knew already. Those were the lost children. She prayed that they would soon be returned home. A whole different kind of shiver raced over her when she thought of Lester. She also prayed that he was dead as she sensed he was. He didn't deserve to live. Not for another day…not even another hour. And then she thought of the missing officer.

"Did they find the other officer?" she asked, hoping against hope he was still alive.

"Not yet." Aidan moved away from the table and toward her. "I see no reason why they would keep his recovery a secret. He's likely still out there somewhere."

Close to death.

The words echoed in Darby's skull. She closed her eyes against it, didn't want to know it.

"It may be too late by the time they find him," Aidan said, confirming the awful premonition she'd just experienced.

She turned away from him, hugged her arms around herself. "I don't want to think about it." She closed her eyes and repressed the memories that tried to surface. "I don't want to think about any of it." Running for their lives in the swamp…hiding underwater…finding the children. She just couldn't bear to think about it anymore.

His arms came around her and he pulled her close, somehow knowing just what she needed at that moment. To feel his strength… his love for her.

Love.

She stilled. Her eyes opened and she clung to him, keeping her face pressed to his chest, afraid to let him see what was in her eyes. Afraid he would read her mind as he always seemed to do. But he did care deeply for her. She felt it in her heart. Yet, she wondered if she could trust her heart. It was the same one that had allowed her to fall in love with a stranger.

A stranger who'd saved her life, she added.

He held her close for a long while, not speaking, not allowing the moment to become sexual. It was about comfort and safety…nothing more.

Eventually, he broke the silence. "Was your Mr. Thomas's visit helpful?"

She pulled back and looked into his eyes. "I don't know." A frown nagged at her brow. "The name Richard O'Riley feels somehow familiar to me but that may be coincidence. I may have had a student with that name or I could have met someone in college briefly." She shrugged. "It's just one of those vague kind of feelings."

"What do you plan to do now? There doesn't seem to be a real direction for you to take."

One hand was rubbing her back, slowly, soothingly. It felt so good, made her want to forget about adoptions and men in white coats or those named Richard O'Riley.

She sighed, suddenly weary. But then, they'd scarcely slept last night and this morning's lovemaking workout had been a hell of a cardio adventure.

"I wish I knew where to go from here." She thought about the few pieces of information she had, the name O'Riley and the fact that the adoption had been a private business deal. That really wasn't much to go on. Definitely no direction, as Aidan said.

She tilted her head back and looked at the man who now owned her fragile heart. "Who do you think those men were last night?" She didn't have to specify which men she meant. He knew. The ones they'd been running for their lives from.

"Not Lester, not the police." He lifted one shoulder in a casual shrug. "I have no idea. Perhaps poachers whose territory we'd stumbled into."

She supposed that could be true, but then again he'd mentioned some pretty high-tech gear. Poachers didn't usually walk around equipped with night vision and thermal scans. She wasn't even certain what the latter was.

"But you were worried that they might have night vision or thermal scans. That doesn't sound like your typical poacher," she countered, putting voice to her thought.

His expression closed instantly. The change was so abrupt it startled her.

"That was just a guess," he pointed out. "I have no idea who those men were, only that they represented a threat of some sort."

He was lying.

The realization rocked through her like a devastating earthquake, shattering her hopes and deflating her dreams. It damaged her somehow, made her want to cry when she'd remained fairly stoic through all of this. It wasn't fair. She wanted to keep trusting him, wanted to believe in him. But he had just lied to her. She knew it with utter certainty.

"Let's sit," he offered, tugging her toward the sofa. "We'll sort through this. You tell me everything you remember about your life before you came to live with the Shepards."

Somehow he tugged her thoughts away from the worry of whether or not she should still trust him. He urged and soothed until she repeated what she'd already told him about the men in the white coats, doctors maybe. All the poking and prodding, tests of some sort. He listened without comment, his expression never altering from that neutral one he'd adopted the moment she questioned him about the men who'd been chasing them last night.

"The only other thing is the word Center," she concluded. "Whether it means anything or not, I don't know. Instinct tells me it's a place…a clinic or something like that. But I can't remember any more than that."

He nodded, then inclined his head to the right. "Have you remembered these details more recently or have you known them all along?"

She thought about that for a bit before answering. "I think I've known some of it all along, but other parts become clearer in the dreams."

"You dream about this place called Center and the men in the white coats?"

"Yes. Not often, but once in a while."

"These dreams frighten you?"

She nodded. "Every time."

This was the part Aidan needed to be sure of. He had to fully understand her intent.

"You feel certain you won't be safe if these men discover your whereabouts?"

She looked directly into his eyes and said what she felt with all her heart, the depth of it glimmering in those lovely eyes. "I think they already know. I think it was them or people who work for them who came after us in that swamp."

He frowned, annoyed at her for persisting, annoyed at himself for losing all objectivity. "What could these men possibly want from you?"

Her head moved from side to side. "I don't know, but I believe it has something to do with this little ESP thing I've got going on." She flushed and shook her head more adamantly this time. "Though I think they'll be vastly disappointed when they discover it only works when it chooses. I have little or no control over it. It'll be just like before. They'll find out how useless my talent is and they'll want to get rid of me."

He tensed as a very specific warning went off in his brain. "How do you mean that?"

"That's why they sent me away," she explained. "At least I think that's what happened. They thought I had some sort of gift and when it didn't work the way they'd planned they sent me away. I ended up with the Shepards."

"You dreamed this?" He had to know how much more she knew or thought she knew.

She drew in a heavy breath and adopted a skeptical look. "Every time I've had one of those stupid dreams, I'm—the me in the dream—certain that if I let them know I have this gift I'll never escape. They'll keep me forever. That's why I pretended it didn't work, so they'd let me go. It was the only way I could escape the place...Center."

Aidan's orders were very specific. He knew precisely how much was too much when it came to what she knew about Center and her past there.

What she'd told him—trusted him with—was far beyond the specified limit.

She had, with her own words, sentenced herself to death.

He could avoid passing on the intelligence to O'Riley for a time. But if she persisted in her attempts to learn about her past, he wouldn't be able to protect her. Telling her the truth would only put her in more danger.

There was only one thing he could do at this point: Keep her distracted until he devised a plan to protect her from Galen, O'Riley and herself.

He reached out to her. She tensed, but didn't avoid his touch. Her reasoning was clear. She knew he had avoided the truth in regard to the men who had pursued them last night. For that her trust wavered. He would have to find a way to reaffirm that trust. To make her forget.

"You've had a long day," he said softly as his fingers curled around her nape. "A long, hot bath would be relaxing." He pulled her to him, claimed her lips. She didn't resist but her hesitancy persisted just beneath the surface. He leaned her back onto the sofa and came down atop her, allowing her to feel the need pulsing already in his body. She moaned softly and he deepened the kiss.

He reached under her skirt and delved into her lacy panties, finding that tight, wet place that burned for him. He knew how she wanted to be touched…knew her most secret desires. He would satisfy each and every one…until all other thought ceased.

Until she was his…completely…once more.

Chapter Twelve

Audubon Zoo
New Orleans

"No, Penny!" Darby rushed to catch up with one of her charges before she got too far ahead of the group.

"Let's stay with the others," she scolded gently. Four-year-old Penny stuck out her bottom lip and trudged back to the group. Though Darby greatly appreciated her new position at the Riverwalk Preschool, she could have done without a field trip her first day on the job. But since she'd missed her real "first" day, she certainly couldn't complain.

Twelve children and three teachers made for nice ratios, but she was still learning the names and faces of those under her care. That made an outing of this caliber less than fun.

The zoo was more crowded than she'd expected. But most of the visitors were groups from nearby schools. As they began their journey into Jaguar Jungle, she quickly surveyed her charges, repeating their names once more. Penny, Jarred, Brooke, Tiffany, and Timmy. No sweat. Two towheads and three brunettes.

She glanced behind her, beyond the clusters of children with their matching shirts that identified their schools and their teachers, who looked flustered already. He was still there. Somehow his presence made her feel safe.

Aidan had insisted that he would hang around a few more days, at least until Lester was found. He wanted to stay close…to make sure she was safe.

The idea warmed her, though she still sensed that he had lied to her about the men who had forced them to run for their lives in the swamp. She could only assume that he had his reasons. Concealing what she suspected could be part of his job. But, somehow, after all they'd shared, she couldn't help feeling disappointed that he'd chosen not to simply tell her that he couldn't discuss the matter. She would have understood. As a teacher, she was well aware of sensitive issues and confidentiality matters.

Directing her attention back to the tour

guide, she dismissed the unsettling thoughts. He would tell her when he could. If he chose not to, there had to be a good reason. She had to trust that. She'd allowed him into her heart…had given her body to him—she had to give him the benefit of the doubt on this, as well. Otherwise, she would be a hypocrite.

She chewed her lower lip and hoped the fact that they'd failed to use protection wasn't going to complicate matters. Though she loved him without question, pregnancy was a subject they had not discussed. Besides, she couldn't be certain he felt the same way she did. She suspected he cared deeply for her. Hadn't missed the way his body responded to hers, the way their lovemaking affected him. But that was not a certainty that he felt the same emotional bond. Her lack of experience in the area didn't give her much of a basis on which to form conclusions. She could only hope that this wasn't a one-sided affair.

She shuddered at the word.

Was it just an affair? It felt like a great deal more than that to her. Desire, strong and hot, sang through her veins each time she thought of the way it felt to be with him. It was too incredible for words. How could that not be true love? Lust couldn't possibly burn this hot.

The children's zoo adventure began with an archaeological dig where they unearthed artifacts that were explained to them in generous detail. She doubted any of them would remember all that the guide passed along, but his dramatic dialogue and presence certainly held their attention well enough.

From there, they journeyed along a meandering path cloaked in fog that reminded her of the cemetery the other night. She thought of the way Aidan had looked in that long duster…like a vampire or a pirate. She shivered and tried again to focus on the guide's narration. The path led through archways, past stone carvings that were realistic replicas of those found in Central America. The whole setting was remarkable.

The real thrill came when they reached the Jaguar Plaza and watched the magnificent cats in a setting that duplicated their natural habitat. The guide talked about their incredible strength and speed. Jaguars were, apparently, afraid of nothing, making them extremely dangerous predators. Darby tamped down another urge to shiver as she watched the sleek animals stalk about before reclining, as if some internal clock had alerted them that it was siesta time.

The children appeared enthralled, pointing and chattering as they admired the beautiful creatures through the sturdy fence that kept awestruck visitors from getting too close. Darby crouched in the middle of her group and observed the show from their vantage point.

Laurie, one of the other teachers from Riverwalk Preschool, was having a difficult time with two of her boys. Darby felt immensely thankful that she hadn't gotten those two. She imagined that they were purposely left off her group since she was new.

"Gage has a kitty just like that at home," Brooke said knowingly. "Same color and everything."

Gage was in Laurie's group with the rambunctious twosome who kept the teacher perpetually preoccupied.

"Nuh-uh," Timmy argued. "His cat's way littler than that. I've seen her. She's just a regular cat, not a *jogwore*," he added, butchering the name for the elegantly lethal creatures.

"Well," Darby interjected before a disagreement could morph into a fight, "what's Gage's cat's name?"

"Harriet," Brooke said. "He named her after his grandma."

"That's nice." Darby smiled, thinking how sweet the little boy was for thinking of his grandmother. She wondered if she…if she and Aidan had children, if theirs would be so nice. She thought of the handsome man and her pulse skittered at the idea of how gorgeous his sons would be.

"I think Gage is gonna be in big trouble," Penny said, joining the amusing conversation. "His momma's gonna be mad as spit."

"Penny," Darby chastised gently, then frowned. "Why would you say that? Did he do something wrong that his teacher doesn't know about?"

The little girl nodded vigorously. "Didn't that man say we wasn't supposed to climb on the fence?"

Darby whipped her head in the direction Penny pointed, just in time to see Gage scramble halfway down the inside of the fence, only to fall from there when his teacher screamed his name. Darby rocketed to her feet and toward the fence. The little boy hit the grassy embankment on the other side of the fence, landing like a cat on all fours, but then he rolled downward right into the jaguar's meticulously arranged home away from home.

Children shouted all around her. The tour guide, looking wide-eyed and as if it might be his first day, too, started shaking his head and repeating the same mantra over and over: you're not supposed to climb on the fence.

Darby flung herself at the fence and started upward, her heart hammering wildly. She had to get to that child. The cats...they would...God, she couldn't even think it. Gage's teacher, Laurie, had grabbed onto the fence as well.

A blur of movement whizzed past Darby. She stalled, blinked and looked again. Aidan was over the enclosure and slipping down the embankment before she even reached the top of the fence.

How had he plowed through all those children and scaled that fence so quickly?

Her fingers clenched around the cold steel as she watched him reach the boy.

Penny's wailing dragged her attention in that direction for a moment. She climbed down and moved to her group, huddling them around her as the scene played out like a bad horror flick.

Aidan had the boy in his arms.

A gush of relief moved through Darby,

through the crowd…their collective gasps and murmurings echoed behind her. *Please, God,* she prayed, *let him get safely out of there with the child.*

Suddenly, the larger of the two cats stood, made a sound that sent a chill down Darby's spine. Her breath evaporated in her lungs.

Aidan stood stone-still. The child in his arms sobbed relentlessly against his chest. She could see Aidan's lips moving, attempting to quietly console the boy.

The cat turned toward them, his fluid movement cautious, deliberate, as he moved between Aidan and the fence. Then the animal froze.

For three excruciating beats, no one moved or even breathed.

In the next ten seconds, two things happened. The cat drew back into a crouch and Aidan burst into action.

The cat lunged.

But Aidan was faster.

New voices behind Darby warned that the zookeeper and security had arrived, but she didn't dare take her eyes off the life-and-death events playing out before them all.

The little boy's arms went around Aidan's neck. He hit the far wall climbing without so much as a split-second's hesitation between running and moving upward. Watching him scale that rock wall was incredible. He didn't slow for an instant, never lost his footing once.

The crowd around Darby burst into applause.

She jumped, startled, then blinked to refocus. He was out…clear of the danger. Safe…with the little boy securely tucked against his chest.

The next few minutes passed in a frenzy of activity. EMTs arrived and took charge of the child, who appeared to be fine except for a few bruises and a skinned elbow. Aidan's hands were skinned and slightly battered from grabbing onto the rough edges of the rocks. A command decision was made by the senior teacher from Darby's preschool—they were out of there.

Aidan smiled at Darby as she, the other teachers and their children filed out of the Jaguar Jungle to head toward their buses. She knew without having to ask that he would follow as soon as the EMT finished cleaning the abrasions on his hands.

As the bus pulled away from the parking lot, Aidan was already climbing into his shiny black sports car as she had known he would.

She didn't look away until the bus had lumbered out onto the street and driven away. Aidan had handled the crisis as if it were an everyday affair in his line of work. Perhaps it was. But he could have been killed. Mauled to death like so many others she heard about in the news.

That was the part that puzzled her—disappointed her. Made her sick to her stomach. How could she have this amazing gift that could locate serial killers and the remains of his victims and not be able to know in advance when a child was in danger...when the man she loved was in danger?

It just didn't make sense.

Maybe her dreams were right. Maybe she was a failure and that's why she'd been sent away from that place after all. The men in the white coats might not even want her. That could be why Aidan seemed so vague and noncommittal about the men who'd been after them in the swamp. It might have nothing to do with her.

Poachers protecting their livelihood or vigilantes after Lester seemed far more likely, now that she thought about it.

Her life wasn't in danger, she decided. Not anymore. Lester wasn't coming back. She sensed that with finality. Though, God knew, she wasn't sure she could count on her instincts in the matter. Yet, somehow, she did. Aidan had said the same. And she did trust him.

Any man who would risk his life to rescue the child of a stranger was a man who could be trusted, in her opinion.

Jackson Square Precinct
New Orleans Police Department

DETECTIVE LANCE WILLIS stood in the men's room on the second floor of the most famous cop building in New Orleans and stared at his reflection. He didn't look that bad for a guy almost forty. He had a few lines, but he didn't smoke or lie around on the beach so they weren't that bad. He'd kept himself fit, still had his hair and teeth. He owned his own house at the edge of the French Quarter and had a fair savings account. He wasn't such a bad catch. And yet he would be forty in three months and he'd never been married. He heaved a sigh and admitted the truth about his martial status. It was tough for a guy to find a wife when his mistress ruled him, his mistress being his work.

The job always got in the way of a lasting relationship. Dames just didn't want their men tied to the job like that. And they sure as hell didn't want some guy that got shot at more often than not. Life was too short to put up with the bull of being a cop's wife.

End of story.

Willis shoved a hand through his hair and headed back to the bullpen. He'd heard about the hero at the Audubon Zoo who'd rescued the child from the jaguars. The man hadn't even given his name but he knew from the description, and the fact that two of his officers were still watching Darby Shepard, that it had been her *friend*.

He hated like hell that he experienced that pang of jealousy. She was a material witness in a case, nothing more. And yet those three days they'd spent practically every minute together had gotten to him on some level. He liked her vulnerability, her innocence. A guy rarely found that these days in the Big Easy.

She was sweet and kind—pretty as hell. He didn't give a damn about her so-called gift. He just liked her. Liked her a lot.

But, according to the officers on her stakeout detail, she'd let her *friend* spend the night in her apartment for the past several nights.

Another pang of jealousy stuck him in the gut. The guy could very well be taking advantage of her vulnerability. Especially right now. She'd been through a lot and needed protecting. Hell, Lester was still out there somewhere.

Willis would find that bastard if it was the last thing he ever did. Find him and send his ass to death row. The remains that Darby Shepard had discovered were still with forensics, but Willis knew they belonged to those missing children. He was certain of it.

He would be the hero when the confirmation came and he could go public with that story. Especially if he nailed Lester in the meantime. He would do that. His task force was not going to fail.

Grabbing a pen he wrote down the name Aidan Tanner. "Chapman!" he shouted across the room. "Get over here."

Chapman, a newbie who'd just been promoted from beat cop after acing the detective's exam, hustled over to see what his boss wanted.

"What's up?" He braced his hands on his hips like a John Wayne wannabe and waited for orders.

"See what you can find on that Aidan Tanner guy who's been hanging around Darby Shepard. I want to know everything you can find on him."

Chapman shrugged. "Ought to be easy enough. She said he's with the FBI."

Shock, followed immediately by fury, boiled up in Willis. "What the hell are you talking about? FBI? Who said he's Bureau? How come nobody told me about that?"

"I thought you knew. He—"

Willis shook his head, cutting off the detective's explanation. "If the Bureau had put him on this case, I—" he jammed his thumb into his chest "—would know it. Bill Frazier is a friend of mine. He's the field supervisor of the New Orleans office. This guy ain't from the Bureau. Not local, anyway."

Chapman shrugged. "Whatever you say, boss."

"Find out who the hell he is," Willis ordered. "Today."

He shook his head. Just who the hell did this guy think he was showing up in his territory claiming to be with the Bureau? Well, if he was a Fed, he wasn't from around here. That only made bad matters worse.

He would get the scoop on this guy and then he'd warn Darby Shepard to beware.

AT MIDNIGHT, Aidan waited in the courtyard for O'Riley's call. Darby had been oddly quiet tonight. She'd fretted over the minor abrasions he'd sustained while rescuing the child who'd managed to land himself in danger. He'd sensed her need to question him about how he'd managed the feat with such ease, but she hadn't asked and he'd kept quiet. He also sensed her disillusionment with her ability to foresee danger. He couldn't explain to her that the talent she possessed required training, honing. It wasn't something she could simply turn on and off at will without the proper skill. And even then, there would be times when life slipped up on her. As it did on him.

Like now.

He became aware of O'Riley's presence outside the gate.

He'd said he would call and Aidan hadn't picked up on anything that indicated otherwise. Obviously he should have.

Aidan slipped through the gate and met his superior on the sidewalk far enough from the streetlight's reach not to be readily visible. O'Riley was a tall man, six-one perhaps. He'd remained lean over the years, but his age was beginning to show in the lines on his face. No one lived this kind of life, certainly not in O'Riley's position, without suffering the consequences.

"I was waiting for your call," he said to O'Riley.

"Since Galen is here, I thought I should be here as well. The decision wasn't made until after I last spoke to you."

Aidan had his doubts about that, but he kept them to himself.

"Tell me what I need to know."

O'Riley was not a fool. He hadn't survived this long in the business by being stupid, either. Though he possessed no special gift of elevated perceptions, his gut instincts were born of experience. Right now, those instincts were telling him that Aidan was holding out on him.

"Lester is dead, I think," Aidan said, avoiding the topic O'Riley actually wanted to discuss. "Galen may have had something to do with that, but I'm not certain."

"What about Eve? Have you determined if she remembers anything as of yet?"

"She remembers nothing," Aidan said without hesitation.

"You're certain of that assessment?" O'Riley returned, openly suspicious.

"I'm certain. We have nothing to fear from her. Our only problem lies with Galen and his followers."

O'Riley studied Aidan for several moments before he responded. "Excellent. I'll be at the Sheraton on Canal Street. Keep me informed of every move you make. If Galen surfaces again, and you know he will, I want to know it ten seconds after you do."

Aidan nodded, then watched him walk away.

O'Riley was no fool. He would not let this go so easily. Aidan had to find a way to make Darby understand how dangerous digging around in her past could be.

Chapter Thirteen

Darby dreamed of home. Of her parents and their first Christmas together.

The Shepards loved her. Gave her everything. Protected her. But even then she had known she had to keep her secret or *they* would come.

The men in the white coats.

She heard their voices as they talked about her lack of progress. Heard the concern regarding failure. One of the men, she couldn't see his face but recognized his kindly voice, worried about her. He feared she would be eliminated.

Another fuzzy image filled her mind in the dream. She had not seen this man for some time. He had left Center. He was cruel and unfeeling. Before he'd gone, Darby had sensed that he would not tolerate her lack of cooperation. She had feared him…just as she feared him now.

He was the man in the white coat who sought Eve.

Eve.

The name felt familiar, made her sad.

Eve had been a little girl at this place called Center—had been afraid…wanted to escape.

Why wouldn't they let her go? Eve was so afraid.

She didn't want to see…didn't want to know.

If she saw, they would keep her forever.

She was Eve.

Darby fought the reality. Didn't want to believe. Didn't want to know. But it was true. Made sense. She wouldn't have the same name now that she'd had then. She had escaped…had gotten a new life and a new name.

She was okay…safe. Aidan would protect her.

She snuggled against his chest, felt his arms tighten around her even in sleep.

He would not let the men in the white coats hurt her. She was safe with Aidan.

The dream turned dark…no, the place was dark. Where was she? Aidan was there. She recognized him, but she was only a little girl. Why was she a little girl in this dream? It didn't make sense. She didn't know this place. An old warehouse on the waterfront. Some place unfamiliar to her. It felt wrong. Threatening. They shouldn't be there. But it was necessary. She had to go…Aidan would not allow her to go alone. He would protect her. She hadn't wanted him to go…had argued with him. Said things she couldn't take back. The hurt hung like a millstone around her neck. She'd tried to push him away. Go! she'd told him. Never come back. She didn't need him. She could do this alone, she'd insisted. There was no choice, really.

If she did not go, someone would die.

Anguish welled inside her.

No.

She didn't want to see.

No.

Don't look.

But she couldn't help herself…had to look. Had to see.

The man wanted something from her… wanted her.

He would have her at any cost.

Aidan held the power to stop him, killed his men one by one. He would win. The man could not stop Aidan…he was too strong… too powerful. He could see just as Darby could.

The man roared at her to come to him. Aidan rushed between them. The man struck…wielding a long knife or sword. Aidan fought him with ease…unafraid. He would win. The little girl…where was the little girl? Aidan's attention shifted at the distraction. In that fleeting moment, the man charged…impaling Aidan with a single blow.

He would die.

Aidan would die before help could arrive.

And Darby would be left all alone.

Eve cried.

Darby sat bolt upright in bed, gasping for air, tears burning her cheeks. A cold sweat coated her skin.

"Aidan!"

"It's all right. Just a dream." He sat up next to her, pulled her into his arms. "You're safe with me."

She hugged him tight, fought the sting of tears. The final moments of the dream played over and over in her mind. Was it just a dream? Or could it be a premonition of what was to come?

She squeezed her eyes shut and refused to

believe the latter. She couldn't lose Aidan, would not even think it.

He held her close until sleep took her again. This time she did not dream…she'd already seen all she needed to.

Her destiny. Aidan's destiny. Nothing she could do would stop it.

INCREDIBLY, Darby had been able to put the awful dream out of her mind as the day passed. Between getting her bearings at the preschool, learning the names of the students and teachers and retelling the zoo story to half a dozen parents, she'd scarcely had time to dwell on the dream or what it did or did not mean.

Aidan had popped in at lunch. Though he hadn't said as much, she sensed that he was hanging around close by. She could feel his presence. It warmed her to know he cared so much, made her want him all the more.

The children had finally gone down for an afternoon nap and she had a moment to herself. Her aide would watch the sleeping angels for fifteen minutes and then Darby would return the favor. She retreated to the break room and enjoyed a cola. For a full ten minutes, she relaxed and sipped her soft drink, content to daydream about making love with Aidan. The intimacy between them was so intense it felt a little scary. She'd never imagined it could be that way… certainly not based on her previous experience—all two times.

What she and Aidan had was special. But what would become of their relationship when Lester was caught and Aidan no longer had any legitimate reason to stay? He would be assigned to a new case and she would be left behind.

An ache pierced her and she had to blink back a wave of tears. Would he ask her to go with him? Would he consider staying? She loved New Orleans…didn't feel complete when she ventured too far from home. But would this eclectic city be all she needed to keep her happy?

No way.

She wanted Aidan in her life. Didn't want this to end.

Today, she decided. When she got off work this evening they would have to talk. She wasn't going to ask for a commitment, just some indicator of what he wanted or where he saw this relationship going.

She loved him. Mistake or not, it was what

it was. Every instinct told her that he felt the same way, but she couldn't seem to trust her instincts these days so that gave her no comfort.

Her ten minutes up, she went to the bathroom and freshened her lip gloss, ran a brush through her hair. Afterwards she returned her purse to her new locker in the ladies' lounge and headed back to the class of four-year-olds where she'd been assigned.

A man waited at the door.

Her forward movement stalled and her heart lunged into her throat.

But when he turned around, she recognized him and relief slid through her.

"Detective Willis, what're you doing here?"

Dumb question, she considered belatedly. He was here about the case, of course. The relief she'd felt suddenly hardened into fear.

Had Lester struck again?

That was her worst fear where he was concerned. The thought that he might harm another child tore at her insides. But he was dead, wasn't he? She sensed that he was… but could she trust her senses?

A resounding no echoed through her brain.

The only thing she could really trust in any of this was Aidan's word.

Only that once had she doubted him and she'd rationalized that incident to the point of completely setting it aside.

"We need to talk. Privately."

The detective's solemn expression sent a new kind of uneasiness slipping over her nerve endings. This did not sound good at all.

"Sure." She poked her head in her classroom and warned her aide that she'd be a few moments more, then she led Detective Willis back to the break room.

"Shall we sit?" she asked, thoroughly unnerved by his somber demeanor.

"You might want to."

Darby took a seat in the closest chair, her knees having gone weak with his words. "What's wrong? You're scaring me."

"We discovered Lester's body this morning."

Relief soared once more. She exhaled a mighty breath of it. "That's good, right? Where was he found?" The whole city would rest better knowing that bastard was dead and, no doubt, in hell.

"He was deep in the swamp. Not that far from where we found the remains. But he was hidden in such a way that it took a team of dogs to find him."

The sound of the dogs barking flashed in her mind but she forced it away. Didn't want to see, or even imagine, the horror of it.

She scrubbed her hands over her face, suddenly weary. Though she felt profound relief at knowing it was over, something nagged just beneath the surface of her newly found calm.

"I want you to see this."

Darby hadn't even realized he'd been holding a large envelope, the nine-by-eleven kind that would hold letters without having to fold them, until he offered it to her. Or photographs, a little voice added.

She took the envelope, her hands suddenly shaking. She banished the foolish trepidation. What was wrong with her?

After opening the clasp, she reached inside and pulled out a thin stack of glossy eight-by-tens.

Her breath left her chest in a rush as her brain absorbed what her eyes saw. Lester… executed in a gruesome fashion.

He was going to die…slowly…painfully.

The thought rammed into her mind, reminding her of what she'd felt coming out of that swamp.

She had known this was going to happen.

"We found my other officer, too," Willis

said quietly. "He's still in a coma but the doctors think he's going to make it."

Her gaze lifted to meet Willis's. He towered over her, his expression accusing. "How did this happen?" Not that she regretted for one moment Lester's horrible death. He'd deserved it. Her jaw clenched at her own hardheartedness. But it was true. The bastard had murdered at least seven children. He deserved this—she glanced back at the photograph in her hand—and far worse.

"We don't know how it happened. The only people we know of having been in the swamp at around the approximate time of Lester's death are you and your friend."

Darby blinked, startled at the implication of his words. "What are you implying?"

He sat down beside her, his expression softening just a little. For the first time since she'd made Detective Willis's acquaintance, she felt a little uncomfortable in his presence. He had stronger feelings for her than he should.

She swallowed back the anxiety building in her throat and struggled to hold his gaze.

"I'm not saying you had anything to do with this," he amended gently. "But your friend is another story. What do you really know about him?"

She shrugged, gave her head a little shake. "What's to know? He's my friend. He's been protecting me."

"Are you completely certain about that?"

Annoyance flared. "What are you trying to say? He's with the FBI. You must know he's been overseeing the Lester case."

Willis wagged his head firmly from side to side. "No, Darby, he hasn't been involved with this case on any official level. He's not with the FBI. In fact, according to every database we've checked, which, trust me, was more than a dozen, Aidan Tanner doesn't even exist."

"That's crazy...impossible. Why would you say such a thing?" She wanted to shake him, tell him to stop lying to her, but she couldn't. Because every neuron in her brain understood that this man was telling her the truth.

"The only hit I got on any search we initiated was from Interpol. Even they don't know who he is, but a man matching his physical description rescued a political attaché in Brussels last year. According to the report, he came out of nowhere and saved the man from certain death amid a hail of bullets and an explosion that no one should have survived. Sound familiar?"

She knew he referred to the daring rescue Aidan had pulled off at the zoo the day before.

He waited a moment for her to respond, but she couldn't. Her throat had closed and her stomach had clenched so tightly she could scarcely keep from grabbing her middle and doubling over with the pain.

"I don't know who this man is, but he isn't from any law enforcement agency we can find. He may or may not have killed Lester. Personally, I don't give a shit. The bastard is dead. The taxpayers won't have to foot the cost of his trial or his wait on death row. He's certainly done nothing wrong that we can pin on him. If we risk questioning him, that'll only give away what we know. The only reason I'm telling you this is because I'm worried about you. Why did this guy pick you? There are serial killers running around wreaking havoc all over the country. Why you? Why Lester? There has to be another connection besides Lester. Do you have any idea what it is?"

A shaky breath rushed into her lungs, an

autonomic response for sure since she couldn't even remember to breathe. "I…I don't know," she stammered. She didn't know anything it seemed…except one thing.

She had to get out of here.

Had to…now.

"Thank you, Detective Willis." She stood on shaky legs. "I have to go now."

He took the envelope from her cold hands and stuffed the photographs back into it. "Call me if you need anything. I'll keep that security detail watching your apartment for a few days more," he added kindly.

She watched him walk to the door. He hesitated before exiting the break room. "Let me know if you need anything at all, Darby. I want to help you."

He did. She knew he did.

But there was nothing he could do to help her.

Nothing anyone could do.

HIS COVER was blown.

That evening as Aidan drove Darby home, he knew with complete certainty that Detective Willis's visit had been about him. He'd seen the man arrive and enter the preschool. He'd come to deliver the news about Lester's death. No surprise to him or Darby. Galen's doing, no doubt.

Willis had been checking into his background. O'Riley had called and warned him that NOPD had initiated a background search. Nothing Aidan hadn't expected. In reality, he was surprised it hadn't happened sooner. But Detective Willis had been too caught up in the manhunt for a child killer to worry about who or what Aidan was.

But now the cat was out of the bag.

Aidan had a decision to make.

Lie to her or tell her the truth.

Both options carried grave repercussions.

If he lied to her, she would know it and would send him away. If he told her the truth, Center would likely eliminate them both.

There had to be a way.

He knew O'Riley was already on to him. Again today, he had asked if Eve had told him anything more. When Aidan told him no, O'Riley had recognized that it was a lie.

Lester was dead. He had no more excuses for hanging around, to Darby's way of thinking. O'Riley was suspicious already. The truth looked more and more like the best option, but it was a noturning-back course of action. Once he'd told her, there would be no way to take back the knowledge that would get her killed if she reacted the wrong way.

It was the only chance he had.

He had to take it.

He followed a silent Darby to her apartment. Once inside, she greeted her cat in that sweet singsong voice, then rounded on him.

"I want to know who you really are," she demanded, fury making her eyes glow with fire.

"All right."

She looked startled, as if she'd expected a fight.

He sat down in one of the chair's facing the sofa and waited for her to take a seat there. He needed the distance the small expanse of floor and the coffee table between them would provide.

"I came from this place you recall as Center."

She trembled, but didn't make a run for it as he'd feared she might do.

"The dreams you've experienced for so many years have a basis in truth."

"Explain," she ordered, unable to wait even a second for the full explanation.

"You and I are the same. We were created

at Center. Genetically designed to be superior to other humans."

This was when the denial kicked in. "That's insane." She bounded off the sofa and glared at him. "Do you really expect me to believe that?"

He opened his hands to her, revealing his unmarred palms. "Look closely, Darby."

She leaned toward him, stared at the hands that had touched her intimately only this morning. But her distraction with the pleasure he'd wrought had kept her from noticing that not a single abrasion or cut remained from his rock-climbing adventure just yesterday.

"How did..." Her gaze collided with his and challenge gleamed there. "That proves nothing."

"How do you suppose I know your every thought?" He smiled. "Well, almost your every thought. You block my touch at times."

She blinked, startled. "I...that still doesn't explain what you're doing here or this outrageous story about my being created at that place."

She started to pace, her long hair swinging around her waist as she executed an about-face and started in the other direction.

Her conservative "teacher" garb couldn't hide the sexy, vibrant woman beneath. He couldn't lose her. He had to make her see...to make her understand.

"Doctors Archer and Galen perfected gene manipulation. They designed a team of Enforcers to protect the nation's interests. Each of us—" he placed his hand against his chest "—has our own special abilities. You and I are seers. We can feel disaster coming...can read the senses and, at times, the thoughts of others. Superior strength and intelligence. The ability to heal at an accelerated rate."

He could see her remembering a childhood without illness, a broken bone that healed overnight. She couldn't deny his words though she wanted desperately to do just that.

She shook her head, pausing in her pacing to stare at him. "I don't have any superior strength. This so-called gift I have is totally unreliable. How can you say we're the same?"

"You merely lack the training and education I have. You haven't been properly instructed in the art of focusing your gift. That's the only difference. Your superior strength has been restrained all these years, but it's there. You are special, Darby. Not like others."

"Just stop," she fairly shouted. "I don't want to hear this. Center isn't a good place. It's bad. They wanted to keep me prisoner…they're still looking for me."

He drew in a deep, fortifying breath, gathered his thoughts before continuing. "It's true that we are not allowed to leave Center as children. But it's necessary for our own protection. If the rest of the world discovered our genetic superiority, we would be looked upon as lab rats to be analyzed. The ability to design superior beings would fall into the wrong hands and mankind as we know it would collapse."

Darby shook her head and huffed her disbelief. What he expected her to believe was totally insane. Sci-fi city. How could he believe such nonsense? She refused to consider that his hands, had, in fact, healed overnight without leaving the first scar.

"Once our training is complete and we reach a certain status, we are allowed to leave Center. We are assigned missions, as I was assigned to this one."

Her gaze tangled with his once more. That was the real reason he was here. Center had sent him. The men in the white coats.

"Why did they send you here?" Willis had been right. This had nothing to do with Lester.

Aidan remained silent for a time. She could see him weighing the words he was about to say.

"Your dreams are right, Darby," he admitted. "When you feigned failure, Center released you from the program. You were mainstreamed into the population and all continued as it should until Lester's case brought attention to the gift you had suppressed." He stared at her for two beats before going on. His eyes begged her to trust him, but how could she? "Dr. Galen," he went on, "was banished from Center years ago. He has worked hard since to bring us down. When your existence was revealed by the media, Center feared that Galen would try to use you against us."

The man in the white coat. "So Galen is one of the men in my dreams wearing the white lab coat," she said, knowing the answer before he replied.

"Yes. He and Dr. Archer. There were others. Lab techs and such."

"Dr. Archer is the one that I sense is kind," she persisted, wanting to know more details.

Aidan nodded, then added, "Was. Dr. Galen saw to it that he was eliminated. He's ruthless, Darby. You must understand how dangerous he is. He wants you and he will stop at nothing to have you."

Her gaze narrowed. He was hiding something from her. "And what exactly is Center's role in this? Why were you sent here?"

He stood and moved toward her. She backed away, not wanting to connect with him on any level until she knew everything.

"I came to protect you from Galen."

"And to see just what I remembered?" she suggested, suddenly certain that evaluating her status was top priority.

"Yes," he admitted. Those dark eyes looked dull with pain. He didn't want to tell her any more, but she would know all of it.

She thought of what Willis had told her about the Interpol incident. These Enforcers from Center were vested with the responsibility of keeping the world safe, in a manner of speaking. She'd read enough thrillers and seen enough movies on the subject to know what happened in cases where their secrets were in jeopardy.

"So Center is this big secret," she commented. "I managed to get loose all those years ago until I suddenly resurface, flaunting the gift I'd sworn I didn't possess. What were you supposed to do if you learned that I knew too much?" That was the key—she felt it so surely that her soul wept with the knowledge.

"If I learned that you posed a security risk, you were to be eliminated."

"So you came here to kill me." The words came out harsh, every bit as cold as the ice currently freezing every muscle, including her heart.

"If necessary." He reached out to her, closed his long fingers around one arm. She couldn't move… couldn't evade his touch. His words had paralyzed her. "Falling in love with you wasn't supposed to happen. I didn't know that they'd created us to be together…that the connection would be so strong. I won't let them hurt you. You must trust me."

How could she trust the man who'd been sent to kill her?

"I want you to leave," she said hollowly, the words lacking any real conviction, but no less clear in their meaning. "Now. Don't ever come back."

"Don't do this," he begged. "I'm the only one who can protect you."

She laughed, the sound dry, empty, just like her soul. "And who's going to protect me from you?"

Before he could answer, the telephone rang.

She turned sharply and strode to the table where it sat at the other end of the sofa. "Hello." The shaky word reflected every bit of the hurt shuddering through her.

There was no hiding the pain…the anger.

"Darby, this is Detective Willis."

She closed her eyes and held on to the receiver with both hands. She didn't want to talk to him right now. She didn't want to talk to anyone.

A rush of energy cut through her, shook her to the core of her being.

"What's happened?" she demanded abruptly, certain that something horrible had occurred…something she had caused.

"Penny Wiseman is missing. She was taken exactly like the others…he left the same flowers behind…but he also left a note."

Goose bumps raced over her flesh. This wasn't possible. Lester was dead. Not Lester, she realized with a sinking feeling that made her sway. "What did the note say?" Her knees tried to give way beneath her, but she fought to hold herself steady. She had to hear this…had to know what she'd missed seeing while distracted by the fight with Aidan.

"He said that he was waiting for you…that you would know the place. If you don't come alone…the child dies."

Fear tightened like a noose around her throat.

She did know…she'd dreamed it just this morning.

Chapter Fourteen

Darby sat in the darkness of Aidan's car. In five more minutes, they would go inside the dilapidated warehouse Galen had selected for this confrontation.

He hadn't called or given specific instructions and though her senses had failed her to a degree, Aidan knew right where Galen was the moment they approached the waterfront. She hadn't wanted him to come with her... still didn't want him here, but she'd needed his power to *see*.

He said nothing but she could feel him watching her, trying to read her thoughts. Well, her ability to *see* might be diluted, as he called it, by her too keen human emotions, but she was still the key to this operation.

Galen wanted her. He would release the

unharmed child when Darby turned herself over to him.

When Aidan's involvement had proven necessary, she had made him swear that he would take the child and leave. He had told her he would, but she wasn't sure she could trust that promise.

It wasn't as if she'd had much choice, since he could see Galen's location and she couldn't.

The matter was simple—she needed him, whether she wanted to or not.

She closed her eyes and pushed away the other thoughts that tried to penetrate her concentration. The memory of making love with him…of his saving her life in that swamp. The way he'd kissed her beneath the water to keep her still and quiet…giving her his last breath.

The tears brimmed instantly and she hated herself for being so weak. Where was that damned strength she was genetically designed to possess? Why couldn't she be stronger than this?

"It's time."

She brushed a tear from her cheek with the back of her hand and faced the man who'd spoken. "This is my show. I say when it's time."

Aidan restrained the need to touch her. He wanted desperately to make her trust him again, but that wasn't going to happen. By the time she realized the truth of his words, it would be too late.

He knew the events that would unfold in that warehouse and he would do all he could to change the final ending. But a part of him sensed that his fate was unchangeable.

He was going to die tonight.

"I'm ready," she said, her voice quivering.

Aidan resisted the impulse to smile. She was so damned strong. Stronger than she knew. Her life would be good. She would make a difference in many ways. The world was a better place with Darby Shepard.

She was out of the car before he could come around the hood and open her door.

"Remember," she said, those sandy colored eyes lifting to meet his, "the moment you have Penny in your arms, I want you out of there. No deviations. Okay?"

"There's just one thing," he countered. The glimmer of tears in her eyes ripped open his chest and tore out his heart. Never had he known such pain.

She folded her arms and glared at him with even more defiance and disdain. "What's that?"

He kissed her…pulled her against him. He

didn't care who watched...didn't care how angry the move made her. He could not die without kissing her one last time.

She tasted so sweet...so good. He wanted to remember that...to remember her forever...to make her a part of his soul. He'd lost her once; this time, he fully intended to take a part of her with him for all eternity.

The wetness slipping down her face startled him, made him draw back. The hot, salty droplets streamed down her cheeks. "Don't make this any worse than it already is," she murmured woodenly.

He nodded and scrubbed a hand over his face. He couldn't be sure if the dampness there had come from her or from him.

She turned away and started toward the entrance to the warehouse. O'Riley and the team he had assembled were out there somewhere. Aidan had alerted his superior the instant Darby got the call from Willis. A man of great foresight, O'Riley had had a team standing by.

They couldn't get too close, however, for fear of triggering Galen's thermal scans. If he suspected the presence of others, he would kill the child. Aidan's presence was expected. Galen would likely be quite suspicious if Aidan didn't show.

The last thing he wanted to do was disappoint the bastard.

Darby had given Detective Willis a location on the other side of town. The detective would be seriously annoyed when he realized he'd been had.

But it would be too late then.

Aidan climbed the steps of the platform flanking the front of the warehouse ahead of Darby. The smell of decaying fish lingered in the air. Rats in search of nourishment ran this way and that as he took the final step. The ambient sounds of night and the water lapping against the pillars supporting the pier were all that broke the silence.

At the entrance, he faced Darby. "You go in ahead of me. I'll be right behind you."

Darby didn't like that suggestion. Didn't trust him to do what he'd promised. "If you do anything that gets that little girl killed," she threatened, still angry with herself for being so affected by his kiss even now, "I swear, Aidan, I'll kill you myself."

His smile was slow and arrogant, caressed by the moonlight and so damned beautiful that new tears came to her eyes in spite of her anger. He looked just as he had the first time she saw him. Dressed completely in black, including that long, sexy duster that gave him the look of a night creature.

"You have my word that I will do nothing to further endanger you or the child."

She rolled her eyes and made a sound of disbelief. "Like I can trust anything you say."

He took her chin in his hand and forced her to look at him. "You can trust me, Darby Shepard," he said firmly. "Remember that always."

She pulled free of his touch. Dammit. Why did he have to make her feel that way? She wanted to stay angry with him...wanted to hurt him the way he'd hurt her.

"Whatever," she muttered and turned back to the door.

Darby took a breath and firmed her courage. Time to face the music. Penny was counting on her. If Galen wanted Darby, he could have her just so long as he didn't hurt that little girl. But the moment that child was out of harm's way, Darby intended to kill that bastard...or die trying.

A flash of light stabbed deep into her brain; images from her dream last night followed hot on its heels. She was in the warehouse... watching. The little girl in her dreams hadn't been her...Penny. It was Penny. No one left but Galen. A pain pierced her chest...Aidan. The image of him being stabbed through the chest exploded in her mind.

It was all coming true…just like she'd seen it.

Oh, God.

"You can't come in." She whirled around to demand that Aidan leave right now. "You have—"

He was gone.

She hadn't heard him move…hadn't sensed his absence.

A chill permeated her being, sank all the way to her soul. He was already inside… *killed his men one by one.*

It was happening exactly as it had in the dream.

She had to stop it.

Inside the building was silence. The two-story structure had seen better days, felt as old as time. An image of pirates hiding their booty flashed in her mind. She swallowed back the fear climbing into her throat. She had to be strong…brave. Penny's and Aidan's lives depended upon her.

Rats scurried across the old wooden floor, their feet making a sound that sent a shiver up her spine. She hated rats.

Her heart thumped violently against her

sternum. She allowed the image of Aidan and the way he touched her…kissed her to distract her mind from the fear. She would not be afraid. Aidan loved her…she knew he did. All they had to do was survive this night.

Aidan would die before help arrived.

She denied the voice that whispered through her mind. No, he would not die. She would not let him die.

Your life is in grave danger.

Madam Talia's voice.

She'd been right.

So damned right.

Large wooden crates were stacked two and three high all around the enormous room. She moved through the rows of crates, her gaze sweeping left to right. She turned down an aisle and stumbled.

A body.

Her breath caught.

A man in black combat gear lay sprawled in the aisle, his neck twisted at an odd angle.

He was dead…Aidan had killed him…*one by one*.

It had begun.

She wove her way between the stacks of crates, moving toward the rear of the warehouse. To where Galen waited with the child.

She could feel his presence now. She hadn't even seen him and she hated him already.

The next stack of crates she cleared brought her into a wide clearing where a couple of desks cluttered with papers stood. Her mind immediately flashed the image of shipping clerks working madly at the desks. Carts sat here and there, loaded with the necessary supplies, including box cutters, twine, drill drivers, hammers, pry bars and varying lengths of steel for bracing items to be packed.

On the far side of the open space, a man stepped out of the shadows to stand in the fringes of the light. The little girl was at his side. She whimpered but didn't dare move. He'd rigged her in such a way that if she moved the rope looped around her tiny neck would tighten.

For a mini-eternity Darby couldn't move or speak. She could only stand there and look at the man who had created her. The picture of him wearing a white lab coat superimposed itself over the image before her.

He was the man who had haunted her dreams all these years.

He was pure evil.

She wanted him to die screaming just as Jerry Lester had.

"I'm here," she said, moving a step closer. "Let the child go."

He laughed, the sound rumbled up from his chest. "Of course. We did have an unspoken bargain, after all."

He picked up a box cutter from the nearby shipping cart and cut Penny loose. She ran immediately to Darby, clutched at her legs.

Darby crouched down, blinking back her tears. "Listen to me, sweetie, you have to run. Okay? Do you understand?"

The little girl shook her head, her own tears spilling anew down her pale little cheeks.

Darby swallowed back a sob. "Run until you find your way out of here. Don't look back. Just keep running, do you hear me?"

Penny nodded jerkily.

Darby stood and gave her a little push. "Run!"

The child did as she was told, not once looking back.

Darby faced the man not more than a dozen feet away. "What now? You wanted me. I'm here."

"Where's your mate?"

Her mate? *I didn't know they had created us to be together.*

Aidan had been right. They had been created to be together. That's why the bond...the connection was so intense. Why she'd never been able to feel complete with anyone else.

"He's here somewhere," she admitted, knowing Galen would spot a lie. "I suggest we make whatever exit you had planned right now."

"I agree." He motioned for her to come to him. "Let's not waste any time."

She moved toward him, taking her time, keeping her gaze glued to his. "Why me?"

He smiled and she had to repress a shudder.

"I took special care with you and Aidan. None of the others are as special as you."

"Really, and how is that?"

She doubted this son of a bitch was capable of anything special.

"I was the sperm donor in your case," he told her bluntly. "You're my child. Of course, you would have to be special."

Revulsion crawled over her skin. "You're nothing," she lashed out. "And I'm definitely nothing to you. The only thing I want is to see you dead," she snarled.

His smile dimmed. "That will change in time." He cocked an eyebrow. "If you want to live."

She strode straight up to him then. "I'd rather die than be a party to your evil machinations."

"Don't make any decisions you'll regret, Eve," he warned.

Eve. The name echoed through her soul. A dozen vivid flashes of memory jarred her mind. She'd been called Eve…back then. The first female. The only female.

Galen grabbed her by the arm and tugged her closer. "It's time to go."

"Not just yet."

Darby's attention snapped to the right at the sound of Aidan's voice.

He approached slowly, deliberately from behind a stack of crates.

Her heart stumbled as her brain assimilated what she saw. He was unarmed. He moved toward where they stood one calculated step at a time, held his arms out so that his enemy could see he was unarmed…nothing hidden under his duster.

"Come any closer and I'll kill her." Galen pulled Darby against him, one arm around her throat, her body positioned to shield his.

Coward. She hated him.

The dream rushed over her senses again, reminding her of what lay in store for Aidan.

"Don't come any closer, Aidan," she cried, her urgency ringing in her ears. "Please, just go."

"I'd take her advice if I were you. I can feel her pulse fluttering wildly. It would be so simple to stop it completely."

"And what about me?" Aidan asked, his face giving away nothing of his thoughts. "You don't want me? The perfect seer you created? I'm sure I would serve your purposes far better than she."

He was going to sacrifice himself for her. She had to stop it.

"Ah, but I can't control you, dear Aidan. You're far too powerful. She's your only weakness. My only hope of escaping. I'm certain O'Riley and his men aren't far away."

Aidan smiled. The sinister expression made Darby shiver. He wasn't going to back off…wasn't going to stop for anything.

"Do you really hope to escape?" Blatant amusement colored Aidan's tone. "You've failed, Galen. It's over."

His face red with rage, Galen shoved her aside…something slid free of his sleeve.

Aidan lunged for him.

"Miss Darby!"

Penny.

Darby swiveled toward the sound of the child's voice.

"I can't find my way out," she cried.

"Run away, Penny!" Darby screamed before jerking her attention back to Aidan. But it was too late…the child's abrupt distraction had prevented her from changing the events she'd foreseen in her dreams.

The world slowed to a crawl. Through a slow-motion lens that narrowed to the point that her vision encompassed only Galen and Aidan, she watched her dream come true.

Aidan was pinned to the wall, his gaze focused on her, the two-foot steel rod protruding from the center of his chest.

He opened his mouth to speak but couldn't. Tried to reach for her but couldn't perform the necessary function.

Darby started toward him, Galen held her back.

"Don't touch him. If he moves even a fraction of an inch, it'll be over."

Arrogantly, Galen moved closer to Aidan, dragging a trembling Darby with him.

She couldn't catch her breath…couldn't

stop the rush of tears flooding from her eyes. She wanted to touch him...to tell him how much she loved him...how wrong she'd been.

"Even now, your left lung has deflated," Galen explained in that tone that lacked any sense of human compassion. "Deep shock will set in soon. Spontaneous breathing will stop. All because of that tiny rupture in the pericardium. Blood will fill it and the heart will be compressed. Full cardiac arrest will follow." He smiled with evil pleasure. "Not even a genetically superior Enforcer can survive without oxygen."

Darby pulled free of Galen and reached out to Aidan, not daring to touch him. "Don't you die on me, Aidan." Galen grabbed her by the hair and yanked her back. "Don't let him win."

She heard the storm of boots and knew help was descending upon the warehouse. She prayed they wouldn't be too late to save Aidan.

"You failed after all, you bastard," she hurled at Galen. "Aidan called his friends."

Galen didn't bother with a response, instead he lifted a section of the wooden floor where they'd been standing moments ago. Darby tried to make sense of his intent, but her gaze kept going back to Aidan. Pain wrenched her soul...she couldn't leave him like that. She had to help him.

The opening in the floor dropped to the water beneath. The sound of an engine revving to life shook her. The pier and warehouses had been built over the water. This was his getaway vehicle.

He was going to escape again.

She had to stop him. She reached toward the nearby cart, her fingers grappling for a weapon. He'd killed Aidan. She wasn't about to let him get away with it.

Her fingers wrapped around a small, cold metal object just as Galen jerked her toward the escape hatch he'd devised.

They went down together.

Hit the icy water in a violent splash.

She struggled to free herself. He held her tighter. She gripped the weapon in her right hand and fought to free that arm...had to do this...had to end it now.

As they bobbed to the surface of the water, her arm came loose from his hold.

She reared back and came down in one slashing stroke with all the strength she possessed.

Galen's throat split open like a gruesome

grin. Blood spewed in her face, the heat of it fueling the vengeance searing her very soul.

She'd killed the son of a bitch.

In a final spasm of action, his fingers locked around her throat. His weight dragged her down, down, down through the crimson-colored water.

She flailed, fought to pull loose from his weight. Couldn't get free…deeper…deeper she sank.

She was going to drown.

Hold your breath.

The words filtered through her soul and she relaxed.

Aidan was with her…

Chapter Fifteen

Center Ghost Mountain
Three days later

"Darby, surely there's some way I can persuade you," O'Riley urged sincerely.

He'd spent the better part of the morning attempting to talk her into reconsidering her decision. She'd gotten the grand tour of Center, even the restricted areas. She'd remembered some parts…could recall being there. But none of it made her want to stay.

That wasn't happening.

"I appreciate your offer, Director O'Riley, but I have a life back in New Orleans. I can't be what you need me to be." Her neighbor had returned from Hawaii and was catsitting Wiz.

She wasn't about to lose anything else. She'd given up too much already.

"The world here at Center has much to offer," O'Riley tried once more. "You'd pick back up with your training, join the ranks of the Enforcers. You're special, you know. The only female."

She closed her eyes and blocked Galen's voice ringing in her ears. He'd said she was special…that she was his daughter.

"I need to go back home." She leveled her gaze on O'Riley's. "Can you understand that? I have to put all this behind me." She shuddered. "Especially Galen."

O'Riley nodded. "I understand. I guess there's nothing else I can do to change your mind." He looked directly into her eyes. "Do you understand what that means?"

She had a pretty good idea. Aidan had told her that security risks would not be tolerated. The only question was how they planned to eliminate her.

"I think I do."

O'Riley's solemn expression turned to one of amusement. "I'm not sure you do, Miss Shepard."

His sudden change confused her. "Why don't you spell it out for me then, Director O'Riley," she said pointedly. If they planned to kill her now, she'd just as soon know. After all, he had given her the full tour. She definitely knew too much now, including their location.

"That means that I have no choice but to permanently assign an Enforcer to guard you and…" he shrugged "…to keep you in line."

Her heart rate picked up with the anticipation surging. "Do I get a say in the matter?"

He shook his head purposefully from side to side. "Afraid not. Aidan is the only one I would trust with this mission."

Her heart leapt. She threw her arms around O'Riley and hugged him tight. "Thank you," she managed to blurt between the tears. "Thank you so much."

He drew back and looked down at her. "Just remember," he qualified, "I might need one or both of you sometime. You have to be prepared to pay back this huge debt."

She nodded and swiped the dampness from her cheeks. "Anything. Anytime. Anywhere." She hugged him again. "You just name it."

"Why don't we see if Medical has lifted the No Visitors restrictions on Aidan. I'm sure you're ready to see him by now."

She nodded again, too overcome to speak. EMTs had come to Aidan's rescue back at the warehouse. He'd gone into cardiac arrest three times before they got him to the trauma center. Thankfully, a cardiac surgeon had been at the hospital just finishing up with an emergency bypass. There had been no time to stabilize Aidan; they'd had to rush him to surgery to repair the damage.

Surviving that kind of injury was slim at best. But fate had been watching out for him that night. The surgeon had already been at the hospital and Aidan was an Enforcer with amazing healing powers.

By morning, he'd been stable enough to transport back to Center where Medical, the most advanced team of medical professionals on the planet, took over his care.

He would fully recover with no permanent damage.

Two members of O'Riley's team had rescued Darby from the water. O'Riley himself had taken out Galen's henchman waiting in the boat.

When they reached Aidan's room, O'Riley hesitated outside the door. "I'm not going to intrude on your reunion. I know you've waited patiently to see him. I won't get in your way. There is one thing I want you to know."

Darby held the man's gaze, not certain she could take any more surprises right now. "Yes."

"Galen told you that you were his biological daughter."

She nodded. "He did, but that doesn't change the fact that I'm glad he's dead." If that made her cold and unfeeling, so be it.

O'Riley chuckled. "That makes two of us. Still, I didn't want you worrying about his claim. It's not true. I will tell you that he attempted to do just that, but I interceded."

Darby couldn't deny the relief she felt at hearing that news. "Thank you. That is a relief."

He patted her arm. "I thought it would be."

He walked away then, leaving her alone to share her wonderful news with Aidan.

A smile pulled across her lips. She couldn't wait to see him. She knocked lightly on the door and pushed it inward.

He lay very still on the bed, the sheets stark white against the bare skin of his shoulders. His eyes were closed and she worried that she shouldn't disturb him. Just then, those dark eyes fluttered open and his lips twitched with a wan smile.

"It's about time," he murmured.

She moved to his side, leaned down and kissed his forehead. She tried to hold back the emotion but it was impossible. "I'm so thankful you're alive," she whispered, lacking the strength to speak at a normal decibel.

"Me, too." He groaned with the effort of moving his arm from under the cover so he could take her hand.

She closed her eyes and thanked God yet again for sparing his life. And for O'Riley's decision.

"You're taking me home with you, are you?" Aidan remarked as if it was no big deal.

A bark of laughter escaped her trembling lips. "Rule number one," she informed him, "no reading my mind unless I give you permission first."

He searched her eyes, his expression suddenly hesitant. "Are you sure this is what you want, Darby Shepard?"

She squeezed his hand gently. "More sure than I've ever been of anything in my life." She kissed his lips. When she would have retreated, he lifted his head to maintain the contact. She lost herself to the kiss…let the feelings flow between them, the heat and the desire. She loved him so very much.

When at last she drew back for air, she said softly, "I'm so sorry I didn't trust you when Detective Willis told me what he'd discovered."

Aidan smiled. "You're only human, Darby. It was a big leap...but you took it in the end. That's what counts."

"So," she said, trying to covertly swipe the moisture from her eyes, "are you sure this is what *you* want?"

"I'd stake my life on it," he said flatly.

Darby laughed. "Not funny."

"I love you, Darby Shepard." He tugged her nearer. "I want to grow old with you."

"Just remember," she said as she positioned her lips mere centimeters from his, "I plan to take my slow, sweet time growing old. We do that down in the Big Easy, you know."

"We'll take all the time you want. We were created to be together."

"I love you, Aidan," she whispered before making the seal of their lips complete. *I love you.* His words echoed softly in her mind.

He was right. They had been created to be together.

This was simply destiny.

O'RILEY OPTED to take the stairs back to his office. He needed to check his messages before meeting Remington for lunch. Afterward, he would brief the Collective and the alert status at Center would be lowered to Secure.

Galen was dead for real this time.

The bastard.

Life was good once more.

O'Riley couldn't think of a single thing that would make this day any better. His mind immediately drifted to the life he'd once had with his wife—ex-wife, he amended.

"Get over it," he muttered to himself. Some things just weren't meant to be.

He'd gotten along without her so far, he'd survived…would likely spend the rest of his life alone.

Heaving a sigh, he pushed the thought aside and entered the spacious waiting room where his secretary held down the fort.

"Any messages?" he demanded gruffly. Everyone expected that from him. He knew the way they talked behind his back. *O'Riley needs to get laid. Ever since his old lady left him he's been a royal pain in the ass.*

Screw 'em. He was still the boss.

"Ah…sir…you have a visitor," his secretary said hesitantly.

O'Riley glowered at her. "You know I have a luncheon appointment. Who the hell is it?" He glanced around the lobby and found it just as empty as he'd thought it to be when he walked in.

"She's waiting in your office." His secretary quickly turned back to her computer, determined not to say more.

Who the hell would just show up at his office?

A woman at that?

One of the technicians or researchers, he presumed. Just what he needed, a bitch session before lunch. They needed this or so and so had done that.

Why did he keep doing this job?

No one appreciated a thing he did.

Well, except maybe Darby Shepard and a few others he'd helped along with their lives. He had to admit, though, that with her he'd had a personal stake in the matter.

When he'd told her that he'd intervened in Galen's attempt to create an Enforcer using his own sperm, he hadn't lied. The truth was, Darby Shepard was his biological daughter. But that didn't matter to her right now. She was completely focused on Aidan. That was okay with O'Riley. He'd tell her someday. Maybe he'd even tell Aidan that Daniel Archer had been his biological father. His assignment in Brussels hadn't been the only reason O'Riley hadn't been able to put Aidan on the Archer mission. That kind of move would have opened up a whole other can of worms, since Archer's daughter was his half sister. It was best not to go there right now. Some secrets needed to be kept.

Aidan and Eve—Darby—would end up married and starting a family, he imagined. Considering one child of an Enforcer had already been delivered and a second was on the way, in the White House at that, Medical might have to set up an entire new section dedicated to studying the offspring. No, he amended succinctly. Not on his watch. There were some aspects of life no one, no matter the reasoning, had a right to touch.

He opened the door to his office and stepped inside, ready to play sounding board. As he closed the door behind him, his gaze lit on the back of a blond head. The woman sat in one of the chairs flanking his desk with her back turned to him. That she didn't bother to turn around annoyed him. He was the boss and deserved a little respect. He tried unsuccessfully to think who on his staff had shoulder-length blond hair.

Before he could come up with a face or name, the woman stood and turned toward him.

Remarkably it was Angela…his ex-wife.

"Richard," she said humbly, more humbly than he'd known her to be in more than a decade. "I've been thinking," she went on, those lovely blue eyes settling on his, her hands sliding into the pockets of her trench coat, "that maybe we should try again."

He snapped his gaping mouth shut and grappled for his voice. What the hell? He'd made that suggestion over a year ago. He'd even felt stupid afterwards when she shunned his offer. Was this some sort of trick? What had changed her mind? His first instinct was to go on the defensive, but he had to give her the benefit of the doubt. She deserved that much. And, God, she looked good. He searched for the right words to say…but rational thought eluded him.

She sighed when he remained silent. "I know I've been unreasonable, but the truth is…I miss you." She said the last with a vulnerability that startled him. He blinked, certain he'd imagined it.

"I'm lonely and I miss you. I need you in my life." A spark of defiance glittered to life in her eyes. "I still think this place is your damned mistress," she stated more forcefully with a quick glance around his office. "But..." She tilted her chin up with mounting determination. "But I can live with that as long as I'm your *wife* and you come home to me at night."

"Angela, I..." This was everything he'd dreamed of hearing from her. But what if he said the wrong thing...made her change her mind. "I never wanted to lose you."

"Then let's forget about the past," she urged, a genuine smile trembling across her lips. "Let's start fresh." As he watched, she shouldered out of the trench coat. She was nude beneath...her body just as beautiful as it had been all those years ago the first time he'd made love to her...the night he'd fallen completely in love with her.

He swallowed at the lump in his throat... somehow he made it to the desk, landed right between those luscious legs. She kissed him hard on the mouth, he groaned with the pleasure of it.

"Are you glad to see me, baby?" she murmured in his ear.

He fumbled for his phone, pressed the intercom button. "Cancel my appointments for the afternoon," he ordered, then turned his full attention back to the woman who'd just blown his mind completely…who'd just made his every fantasy come true. "Tell me I'm not dreaming," he murmured, unable to take in enough of her. His eyes couldn't move fast enough, his brain couldn't comprehend—she was so beautiful and she was offering to be his again.

She grabbed him by the necktie and pulled him to her. "You're not dreaming. I was wrong. It just took me a while to realize it. Now let me show you how much I want you." In a preview that hardened every muscle in his body, she traced a path around his mouth, along his jawline with that talented tongue.

He kissed that luscious mouth. "Why don't I show you first?" Before she could argue, he showed her over and over again. On the desk. On the floor. Against the wall. He might be pushing the far side of fifty but he wasn't dead.

When they both gasped for breath, he kissed the woman he loved and smiled.

He'd gotten a second chance.

He didn't intend to screw it up this time…she would never lack for his attention.

"Is that clear enough?" he asked when she'd come for the umpteenth time.

"Oh, baby," she said on a delicious sigh, "I've missed you. Come home with me and I'll take my turn." She trailed a red-tipped nail along his still fully aroused length.

"Gladly," he assured her. He would take her home and never again would he consider this place his home. Home was where the woman who loved him—the woman he loved—lived.

A sappy grin cut across his face. He had a brand-new motto: saving the world began at home.

* * * * *

*Look for Debra Webb's
next Harlequin Intrigue,
URBAN SENSATION,
coming in August.
Then in October look for Debra Webb's
COLBY CONSPIRACY
from Signature Select.*

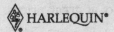

Emotional, compelling stories that capture the intensity of living, loving and creating a family in today's world.

Modern, passionate reads that are powerful and provocative.

Romances that are sparked by danger and fueled by passion.

SILHOUETTE *Romance*

From today to forever, these love stories offer today's woman fairytale romance.

Action-filled romances with strong, sexy, savvy women who save the day.

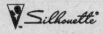

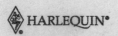

INTRIGUE

Return to

MCCALLS' MONTANA

this spring
with

B.J. DANIELS

Their land stretched for miles across
the Big Sky state...all of it hard-earned—
none of it negotiable. Could family ties
withstand the weight of lasting legacy?

AMBUSHED!
May

HIGH-CALIBER COWBOY
June

SHOTGUN SURRENDER
July

Available wherever Harlequin Books are sold.